I0595077

THE MOON TOUCHED CHRONICLES

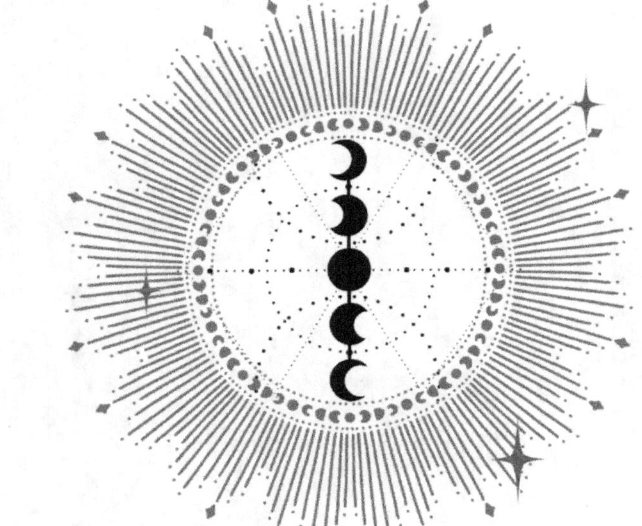

Nightfury

RUBY ELLIS

For the dreamers.

I hope you are always courageous enough to reach for the

stars and hold on tight.

Content Warning

This book contains strong language, sexually explicit scenes, discussions of drink tampering, violence, kidnapping, child neglect, poisoning, societal infertility, pregnancy, childbirth, and loss.

Table of Contents

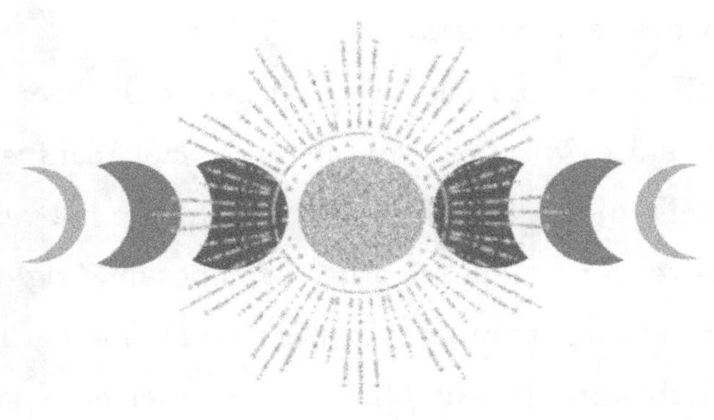

Chapter One

"This is Juniper," I explained. "She is mine."

I had planned so many different ways to tell my sisters about Juni but walking into the kitchen—seeing them for the first time in months—I completely forgot the thought-out introduction that I was going to use and instead uttered a simple, 'she is mine.' I mentally face-palm and tack on a smile in hopes that this isn't as awkward as it seems. But it is. I know that it is. Because we are standing in a kitchen, surrounded by people who were definitely not expecting us to waltz in with a child, and not a single breath can be heard. Not even my own.

The air has been completely sucked out of the room until Ramsey breaks the silence.

"How is that possible? It has only been a few months since we last saw you." Her confusion is completely understandable. But I still have not regained control over my tongue. Words are impossible right now.

Standing next to Ramsey is a large man with short, brown hair and piercing blue eyes. He looks at her like she has hung the moon.

She steps closer and tucks a strand of my wild hair behind my ear. That is when she notices the markings on my temple. She looks at the little girl in my arms and then turns to Bade. She sucks in a sharp breath as she notices the matching marks on his face.

"Moon Touched." Her words are barely more than a whisper. Revered.

Ramsey shows me the marks on her hands while Rowan steps forward and pulls the neckline of her dress down. She has the marks too. Taking a closer look at the men who must be Bade's brothers, Warrick and Griffin, I see that they have matching markings with my sisters.

"And there were three, goddesses of the moon," the brother whose marks match Ramsey says.

"Are you Mated?" the other brother asks. His marks match Rowan's. He is just as tall as Bade, with shoulder length black hair and blue eyes that match both brothers.

There is another man in the room who looks slightly older, though it is hard to tell with their extended lifespans. His eyes are green, but he has dark features like Ro's Mate.

"No," Bade and I answered at the same time. It comes out a little harsher than I mean, but it is the truth all the same. Bade and I have come a long way to be where we are right now, but we still have further to go on our journey towards whatever we will be.

"We will revisit that later," Rowan says. "Can someone please explain how this adorable little girl is yours? I got knocked up almost immediately after we arrived in this world and my babies are still cooking."

I look down at Ro's swollen belly. She looks like she could be due any day, though admittedly, I do not know much about wolf-shifter gestation.

I am about to speak when Sylas enters the kitchen. Bade told him to wait outside the lodge but his wolf did not want Juni to meet new, powerful people without him present. Bade assured him that she would not be in any danger here, but he had to see for himself. I rolled my eyes as they argued about it on our way here. There are still a lot of things about this world that I do not understand, and the complexities of sharing souls is one of them.

Upon seeing Sylas, the mood in the room changes drastically. All of the warmth I felt when reuniting with my sisters has cooled down to freezing. It is clear that Sylas is not welcome. Ramsey retreats into her Mate's arms while Rowan's Mate shifts into a massive black wolf, positioning himself between Sylas and everyone else.

Apparently, there was cause for concern with this meeting after all–though it seems to have nothing to do with Juni and *everything* to do with Sylas.

"What is he doing here?" Rowan snarls so fiercely that she seems more wolf than human. Bade's brothers must have done that mind communication thing because Ramsey is pulled behind her Mate while a fierce growl leaves his chest.

I look to Sylas, unsure as to what is happening right now. He does not give me any indication that he understands what this is about either. Bade moves so that he is in front of me and Juni, leaving Sylas to stand on his own while he faces more than one angry Alpha.

"How could you bring him here?" Ramsey's Mate asks Bade.

"You need to allow Reese to explain, Griff," Bade replies.

"Reese is welcome to explain, but Sylas needs to leave the lodge right the fuck now," Griffin replies. "War is barely able to hold himself back." War, the wolf, is growling and pacing in front of Ro. She reaches down to touch his back but the look on her face is almost as menacing.

"Why?" I ask quietly. I have no idea what would cause such a strong reaction. I didn't even know that they knew Sylas.

"Because his chosen mate almost killed me and my unborn children a few weeks ago," Rowan says. "He needs to leave before War rips his throat out."

Sylas's face turns white as he steps back to stand in the doorway. "I did not know," he tells them. "I did not know."

"Go wait outside," Bade tells him. Sylas nods his head and backs out of the kitchen. Nobody moves until we hear the front door snick closed.

"Perhaps we should move somewhere more comfortable?" the older man suggests. "War, shift back so that we can figure this out. Your Mate and pups are safe with all of us here."

War shifts back into his human form and moves to stand behind Rowan, pulling her flush against his body.

Griffin opens a cabinet and pulls out a pair of pants for War to put on.

"We keep pants in the kitchen now?" The corner of Bade's mouth hitches up in half a smile.

"I started stashing them around the lodge when Rowan moved in. I do not need her seeing your cocks all of the time," War replies.

"Jealous, brother?" Bade jokes.

"There is no need to be jealous," Rowan jumps in. "You are all massive. I am far more concerned with a bare ass on the sofa situation."

"And nobody needs to get poked in the eye at the dinner table," Ramsey adds.

I can't help the laugh that bursts out of me. I have missed my sisters so much.

We all move into a room with more comfortable seating. Juni has fallen asleep in my arms so Bade gently pulls her away from me and lays her down on one of the comfortable couches, covering her with a blanket. Everyone in the room tracks the movement but don't say anything.

Unlike how my sisters are pulled down onto their Mates' laps, Bade sits down next to me. A pang of jealousy runs through me at the open displays of possessive affection that are shown to my sisters. I am not even sure if I want the whole 'over possessive mate thing'—my feelings for Bade are complicated—but I am jealous all the same.

Shaking off the feeling, I focus my attention on the familiar faces in the room. "Where should I start?"

"At the beginning," Ramsey replies. "We want to know everything."

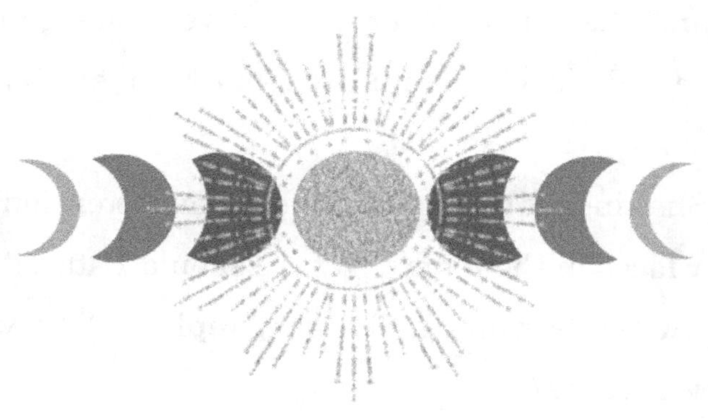

Chapter Two

(Several Months Ago)

I wake up shivering. My entire body is screaming—every muscle feels as though it was shredded and then glued back together. I don't know where I am. I wrack my brain, trying to remember the last 24 hours but my head hurts so badly that I throw up.

I reach for my purse, needing my migraine medicine, but realize that it is not with me. I never leave home without it. How did I get here? I pry my eyes open a little wider, but the sunlight is too bright, reflecting off of the snow. My teeth chatter as I stand. I need to find some shelter—somewhere that I can ride out this migraine and figure out where I am.

Eyes half open, I stumbled around the frozen forest looking for shelter. Maybe there is a road nearby where someone could drive me back into the city. But all I can see are frozen trees, branches weighed down by ice and snow. The ground is freshly covered as well, leaving a blanket of undisturbed earth. No tracks. No paths. No roads.

By the time I find a small cave, my feet are numb from walking barefoot through the snow. If I do not warm up soon, I am going to freeze to death. I might already be too late to save all of my toes from frostbite. Trying to remember what I learned during my wilderness survival class in high school; I make an inventory of my available resources. Snow—that's just frozen water. If I had a fire, I could heat it but until then, I will eat it to stay hydrated.

I look down to see that I am wearing borrowed pajamas. The pants are torn and soaked around my ankles, and the oversized tee is doing little to protect me from the elements. Not ideal, but it is better than being naked. Maybe. Probably.

I don't have any way to make a fire, even if I knew how to rub sticks together or bang rocks to make them spark. Hopefully the cave walls will help keep me warm. Exhausted, I curl up in the corner and fall asleep.

"We are going to have so much fun tonight!" It is Ro's 21st birthday so Rams scored us a table at a popular nightclub. I think she is banging the bartender, though she never discusses her love life with me, so I do not know for sure.

"Are you sure I can be here?" I am only 19. I do not want my sisters to get into trouble for bringing me here. Breaking the rules is not something that I am used to doing. Reese, the innocent one. Reese, the quiet one. Reese, the rule follower. Every hat that I wear is just a different shade of the same, safe color. But it was all that I knew. Entering the foster care system when I was two, I learned to not draw attention to myself. I needed to blend in, be accommodating, not cause any issues so that a family might choose us. It didn't work, but at least I did not suffer any abuse like some of the other kids in the system did.

"It will be fine, Reese. Rams got us a table, and we are mostly going to be there for the dancing." Ro tells me as she holds my hand and pulls me along with them.

Once I show my fake ID to the bouncer, we find our table. Ramsey pulls out a list and orders the drinks that Rowan wanted to try. They all have dirty names. I can't help but blush as the waitress reads our order back to us before handing the ticket over to the bartender. He looks at it and then follows her line of sight over to our table, giving us a wink. That must be the bartender Ramsey is screwing.

When our drinks arrive, we share them all. I take tiny sips since I am not used to drinking alcohol. I have really only had cheap wine before.

We leave our table when Rowan's favorite song comes on and we head over to the dance floor. We promised each other that we would not separate tonight. But after dancing for a long while, that is exactly what happens. I feel hands on my hips as someone pulls me flush with their body. I turn and politely decline. I am not at all interested in grinding up against a random man in a nightclub. He can take his half hard dick somewhere else.

I try to find my sisters in the crowd, but it is just a mass of sweaty bodies, and I cannot see them anywhere. I head back over to our table as I start to feel lightheaded and dizzy.

"Reese?" I hear someone call my name. At first, I think it is one of my sisters, but the voice isn't quite right. A hand grips my arm to catch me as I stumble. She says something else to me and that is when I realize that it is my friend Mia from school.

"What are you doing here?" she asks me, her eyes scanning my face and body as I try to clear my head. "Are you okay?"

"I can't find my sisters. We are here for Rowan's birthday. Have you seen them?" At least, that is what I try to say. My words sound garbled. She must have understood what I was saying though, because she started looking around for them too.

"How much have you had to drink, hun?" I tried telling her that I had about six tiny sips, but my head feels wrong.

"I think someone might have drugged you." But how is that possible? Our drinks came directly from the bartender that Ramsey knows.

Mia calls over some of her friends that she knows from school. Most of them I have seen around campus. They all help Mia look for my sisters. I helped her unlock my cell phone and she was able to find pictures of them to pass around.

I do not know how long I sat there. The world around me is a blur of loud music and movement. My head begins to pound but I can't take my medicine with alcohol

My return to consciousness is slow, like I am wading through syrup. I keep my eyes closed because my head is still pounding. What happened after Mia found me in the club? Where did my sisters go? They would not have left me alone. I know that with every fiber of my being. Did they get drugged too? They must have—we all shared the drinks. That's when I remember where I am. The cold. The forest. The cave. How did I get here? I don't even know where *here* is. Wait...why am I warm?

Risking exacerbating my migraine, I peek my eyes open. I look at the smooth stone of the walls around me—I am still inside the cave. So, that part was real, then. The heat is coming from my abdomen, like I am curled around a hot water bottle. Looking down, I gasp.

My eyes fly open, no longer caring about my migraine, because my body is wrapped around a freaking bear cub and I am worried that its mama is going to come in and make a meal out of me.

How is it possible that I found myself in even more trouble while unconscious? As if the freezing temperatures, no food, no idea where in the actual fuck I am or how I got here, I now get to add claws and teeth to the immediate threats that I am facing.

I try to slowly pull myself away, not wanting to disturb the cub, but it feels my movement and lets out a large yawn. The cub slowly sits up and looks at me. I swear, this cub tilts its head to the side as if it is trying to figure out what I am doing.

I have never been so close to a bear before, but this little cub has to be the cutest thing I have ever seen. Fuzzy brown fur, large golden eyes, I feel like one of those women on TikTok who befriend raccoons and cougars in their backyards in an effort to live out their Disney princess fantasies.

"Hello, cutie." I keep my voice as calm as possible, not wanting to startle the bear. "I promise I won't hurt you. Can you, maybe, please don't let your mama eat me?"

Lord. I am talking to a bear cub. This is definitely the strangest encounter that I have ever been a part of.

"Is this your home?" I ask as if the cub will actually tell me.

In the blink of an eye, the cub changes from a bear into a little girl. A little girl with dark brown hair and eyes that look like liquid gold. A little girl who has been in my dreams since I was a little girl myself.

How is this possible? Am I dreaming right now? That must be it, right? This does not happen in real life.

I reach down to pinch my leg. Ouch! Holy Hannah, this *is* real.

I always assumed that the little girl from my dreams was someone that I had met when I was young. Growing up in foster care, there were many faces that came and went, and I thought that she was maybe a friend that I remembered through my dreams. But apparently not. My little dream bestie is actually a bear cub shifter.

"This innit my home," the tiny voice says. "I know that you won't hurt me, silly."

What is happening right now?

"I think I got lost," I explained, confused. "Do you know where we are?" This kiddo cannot be more than four years old. How is she going to know where we are?

"We are in Nightfury." she says it as if I should know where that is. When I do not say anything, she adds, "Wolf territory."

I have no idea what that means—though she just transformed Beauty and the Beast style from a bear into a child so maybe she does actually know what she is talking about.

"Where are your parents?" I ask. I could really use an adult right now.

"No mama or dada, just me." Her reply is not sad. It is just stated as a fact.

15

"I don't have any parents either," I offer her an understanding smile. "I have sisters, though. Do you have any other family?"

She shakes her head. "Alone. Just me." This time, she does not keep the sadness out of her voice. Her eyes begin to fill with tears and her little lip trembles. She must be so scared to be out here all on her own. How is it even possible that she has survived? She is so young.

When the first tear spills onto her cheek, I reach out and pull her into my arms, enveloping her in a hug.

"We will figure this out together, honey," I tell her against her hair.

I rock her in my arms and rub her back, just like Ramsey would do for me when I was sad. After a while, her tears dry up, but she stays snuggled up against my chest.

"What is your name?" I ask quietly.

"Nana called me Juniper or Juni." Her Nana must be gone too, if she is out here on her own.

"That is a beautiful name. It is nice to meet you, Juniper. My name is Reese."

We spent the next several hours foraging and gathering wood for a small fire. Juniper was able to show me what berries are safe to eat and which ones to stay away from. She also knows how to start a fire. From what she has told me, I believe that she has been surviving on her own for about a year already. Her parents were killed when she was a baby, and she lived with her grandmother until she passed away last winter. Juni's grandmother taught her how to survive off the land and I am incredibly grateful. It is humbling to have to follow the lead of a young child, but it is clear that I am not in New York anymore.

Based on what I have witnessed and learned, I'm not even sure that I am on Earth anymore. Surely if shifters existed on Earth, we would have found out about it by now. Right?

Juni is a little chatterbox, and I find myself laughing as she tells me about herself. She tells me about this world. Her descriptions and explanations are a bit unorganized, messy, but I am able to follow along for the most part—my brain filling in the gaps.

In this world, there are several territories that are divided up by different shifter groups. The larger territories are kind of like countries. Then, depending on the species, the larger territories may be broken down into smaller territories—like the Nightfury territory that we are currently in. The bear shifters, like Juni, live in clans. The clans have been in a bit of a civil war situation for quite some time. That is why Juni's grandmother stole her away from the clans, when her parents were killed, to protect her.

Before her grandmother died, she told Juni that she needed to follow her heart string, whatever that means, further into the wolf territories.

Wolves live in packs, and the wolf shifter territory is divided into three smaller territories. The wolves have Alphas and Betas who govern over the packs–just like in the shifter romance books that I like to read.

There are many other shifters and territories, but the only other one that Juni knows anything about are the panther shifters whose territory shares a border with both the bears and the wolves. She told me that the panthers are very secretive, so her grandmother did not teach her much about them.

By the time we make it back to the cave, both of our stomachs are rumbling. Juni portions out the berries that we found, giving me a larger portion. When I tried to make sure that she ate her fill before I took any, she growled at me and told me that my body needed more energy than hers because of the magic running through her veins.

Giving in, I demolish the pile of berries in front of me. They are both sweet and tart. The juice leaves a sticky residue on my lips and tongue. I wash it all down with some snow that we melted down by the fire.

"Your grandmother told you to come into wolf territory?"

"Nana said to follow my heart string." Juni rubs her small hand over her chest. "My heart string leads me where I need to go to keep safe."

"Is that something that everyone has? A heart string?"

"Dunno. But I have it. I can feel it. It led me here to the cave so that I could find you. Now, it pulls me again."

"Where is it pulling you?"

She shrugs. Juni yawns and then shifts back into a bear, snuggling up next to my side. It isn't long before her breathing evens out and she falls asleep.

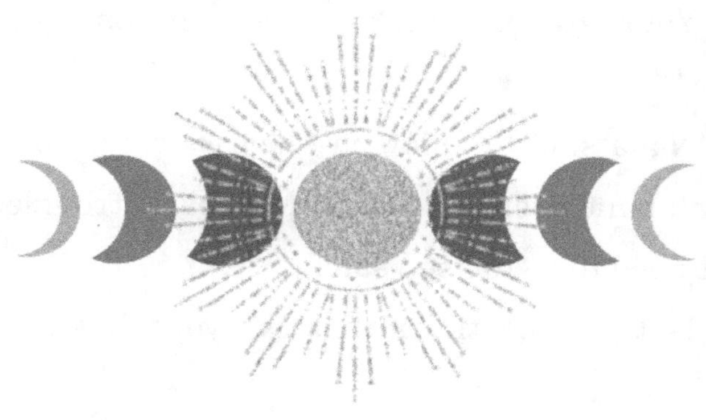

Chapter Three

Juniper and I slowly travel across Nightfury territory and into Nightfang territory. I only know that we have passed from one to the other because Juni tells me. The land is almost exactly the same, though the weather has started to become less frigid.

We spent about two weeks traveling together before we came across a town. Or, an outpost, I guess. We steered clear, not wanting to draw attention to ourselves, but Juni did sneak in to steal a blanket and a flask for water. I did not want her to risk it, but my headaches have been horrendous, and I couldn't stop her.

Luckily, we were able to find another cave to rest in while the worst of my migraine hit. Without my medication, I am almost completely useless. We travel as much as we can at night, avoiding others and the light that often makes my head worse.

Juni has had some success hunting small animals that we can roast over a fire, but we are mostly surviving off of berries and water from the creek or melting snow.

I have lost track of how long we have been traveling. It has been several weeks, though. Maybe even a couple of months. We are following Juni's heart string but are avoiding the outposts that pop up much more frequently now that we are in Nightfang.

While she still shifts to sleep and hunt, Juniper spends almost all her time in her human form. A few times now, we have come across an abandoned sled of supplies or a home that is no longer occupied. Making sure that they are truly abandoned, we take clothing and soap. We use everything sparingly, and I feel bad for stealing the items, but we do not have much choice. We bathe in streams. The water is ice cold, but it is worth the chill if it means being able to wash the layers of dirt and grime off of our skin. Fresh clothing helps too–though it is difficult to find items that fit us.

After what I think is another couple of weeks, we arrived at a small outpost. Juni doesn't know why her heart string brought us here, but she says that this is the place. Staying on the outskirts–we are close enough to see but far enough that we will remain hidden. Juni and I watch as two families go about their day. There is a young boy who laughs and plays while the adults tend to the camp and prepare dinner.

Eventually, we fall asleep in a hidden grove, snuggled together since we cannot risk a fire. Early that next morning, we discovered what was pulling us here–or rather, who.

The sound of Juni growling is the first thing I hear. Before I open my eyes, I can feel her standing over me, protecting me, in her bear form.

"It is okay, little one," a male voice says.

My eyes fly open, realizing that we are not alone. I stand, letting Juni stay in her bear form at my feet.

"Don't come any closer," I warn. I keep my voice firm, despite the fear that I am feeling. The man standing in front of us is at least a foot taller than me. He is lean, though he is still built like an athlete. He looks to be in his mid-to-late twenties, but from what Juni has explained, shifters age at a different rate than humans. He could be hundreds of years old for all that I know. What worries me the most is that his face is familiar too. I have seen him in my dreams before.

"I will not harm you," the man says. I am not reassured at all. Isn't that something that someone who wanted to harm us would say?

"What do you want?" I ask.

Juni shifts back into her human form, pulling her little dress over her head. "He followed his heart string, too," she tells me.

I pick her up, holding her tight to my body protectively.

"Who are you?" I ask the man. He did not appear in my dreams as frequently as Juni did, but he was there often enough that he became familiar.

"My name is Sylas," he tells me. "Are you at all related to Rowan? I met her while she passed through with the Alpha. She speaks the same language as you."

My heart begins to beat faster. Rowan? He knows my sister? She is here too?

"Rowan is my sister. Do you know where she is?"

"I believe she is back at the lodge with her Mate. In the main village."

With her Mate? Rowan has a Mate in this world?

"I know that you are not from here," he continues, "but I would be happy to answer any questions that you have."

"Mate...like her husband? Did Rowan get married?"

"Yes, but it is more than that. Rowan and the Alpha are True Mates. The Alpha found his soul within your sister."

"She found her soulmate?"

"Yes. And I have found mine. That is why I am here."

He found his soulmate here? Where I am standing? Surely, he doesn't mean that I am his soulmate.

"You must be mistaken," I tell him. No offense to him but I am pretty sure that soulmates are supposed to know when they find each other and I do not feel anything but confused.

"My wolf is not mistaken. The little girl that you are holding holds the other part of our soul." He says it gently—not wanting to scare me off but what in the actual hell is going on right now? He cannot be serious.

"A little girl cannot be your soulmate. That is ridiculous. She is just a child."

Juni turns my face to her. She keeps her little hands on my cheeks as she speaks. "My heart string led us here. My bear says that his heart pulled mine and mine led me to him," she tells me.

I turn back to face Sylas. "I am going to need you to explain this to me in full detail. This is not something that would ever happen where I am from."

"Wolves and bears both believe in The Mother. Our creator. I do not know much about bear shifters other than some basics, but I can tell you what I know as a wolf. The Mother created all life. Wolves used to run in packs, similar to how we do now, but they did not have a shifted form. The wolves became lonely and asked The Mother for a companion. The Mother split their soul and created our shifted forms. The wolves still felt like something was missing, so The Mother split their soul further and placed it within their True Mate. Their soulmate. We are born separate, and our souls call out to each other, looking for their missing pieces."

"And Juniper is your True Mate?"

"Yes. My wolf has found our soul within hers."

"But she is just a child. You are...not. Is this not weird to you?" Sylas chuckles at me.

"Shifters live long lives. It is not uncommon for True Mates to be a wide range of ages."

"But how will that work? I mean, what will your relationship with her look like? Would you be her guardian?"

"No. You are clearly her chosen guardian. My wolf and I will protect her. We will provide for her. As she grows, we will hopefully become friends. Now that my wolf has found her, our sole purpose is to ensure her wellbeing."

"It is okay, Reese," Juni says as she holds my face in her hands, looking into my eyes. "His wolf will not let him hurt me. My bear says I'm safe."

My head is swimming with all of this information. Even though I have traveled through this world for several weeks, it still feels like this all must be some weird dream.

"And this heart string that Juni told me about…is that the soul call thing that you were talking about?"

"I believe so. Wolves believe that our souls are what pull us together. Bears might refer to it as a heart string. Our power is felt in our chests."

"A Heart Mate," Juni whispers as she wiggles from my arms.

Sylas makes himself smaller, crouching on the ground in front of Juni. "Is that what bears believe in? A Heart Mate instead of a True Mate?" he asks her.

"Think so. I dream when I sleep but Nana was silly and did it when we awake. She told me about Heart Mates after a dream. And said I need ta' follow my heart string when she gone away."

"Your Nana had visions?" I ask.

Juni shrugs. "She was a daydreamer."

I look to Sylas, wondering if this is making sense to him. Is any of this even possible?

"All shifters have magic. We would not be able to shift without it. Some have more magic than others—like the Alphas. I am sure that extra magical gifts also show up in the other shifter species," he explains.

Is that what my dreams were? Do I have some latent magic? My migraines have always caused my most vivid dreams. I always believed that it was a side effect of the medicine that I take when I am battling one. But what if it was this? What if I was meant to be here, in this magical world instead? It is honestly too much for me to think about right now.

"What now?" I ask. "Is it possible for us to get settled in the outpost? Just temporarily." I need him to understand that we will not be making this outpost our home. If my sister is in this world, I need to find her.

"Of course. We keep lodgings available for travelers. I will show you there and then I need to have a conversation with someone in the camp."

My hackles rise. "What does that mean? Will we be safe?"

"Yes, you will be safe. There is someone who I have been spending my life with. Her name is Zuri. She is not my Mate though we have lived that way for a few years. She needs to know that I have found my True Mate."

Well, that sounds like an awkward conversation to have.

"There is another family that lives at this outpost. Fiske and Zya live with their young son Jasper. He is about the same age as Juniper. He will be happy to have another child to play with while you are here. Zya and Zuri are sisters."

"Are they going to be okay with us being here?" I really do not want us to walk into a situation where we are not welcome.

"Of course," Sylas reassures. "Travelers are always welcome."

I held Juni's hand and cautiously followed Sylas into the outpost. Sure, travelers might always be welcome, but we are not typical travelers. We are the reason he needs to break up with someone. He directs us to a circular, yurt style home close to the central campfire.

"Go ahead and get settled. I will return shortly with some food and hot water for a bath."

"Thank you," I say as I enter the tent with Juni. The inside of the home is one large circular room. There is a fire in the middle and a large pallet-style bed towards the back. The room also has a free-standing bathtub and a table with two chairs. The bed is covered in warm furs and blankets. It has been so long since I last slept in a bed.

I open one of the cabinets and find a few pieces of clothing—though it all looks far too large for us. I pull a tunic style shirt out for myself. I can wear it like a dress after we bathe. Maybe Juni can borrow some clothing from Jasper.

Sylas arrives with a tray loaded with food and several buckets of hot water. He also has a small basket with soaps and a smaller tunic for Juni to wear.

"Please do not hesitate to find me if you need anything else," he tells us as he leaves.

"Let's eat while we let the water cool a bit," I say after testing the water with my fingertips and pulling them back sharply from the heat.

The food that was provided is wonderful. I do not know if it is because we have had limited options while we travelled but the stew is hearty, seasoned well, and warms us up from the inside out. The bread is delicious, both on its own and dipped in the broth. There are also berries, nuts, and what I think might be soft cheese. Juni eats her stew so quickly that I give her the rest of mine.

In the bath, I wash Juni's hair, braiding it into a fishtail plait down her back and securing it with a thin piece of leather. There isn't much hope of containing my curls without any product, so I just embrace the wildness and leave it down to air dry.

We fell asleep that night with full bellies, clean hair, and a new sense of safety. It is the first night that I was able to sleep soundly since I arrived in this world.

It was early morning when I woke up to the feeling of my temples burning. It was not a normal headache. And the dream that I had was not a normal dream. It was a vision. I know it in my bones. Images flashed through my mind vividly. Similar to the dreams that I have had since I was a little girl but brighter. More intense. And it has left me with a sense of clarity that I have never really felt before. I look at the little girl who is cuddled up against me and I know what I must do. It is the only way. I saw it.

"Juni," I whisper. "Wake up, honey."

Juni stretches, opening her eyes and smiling when she sees me.

"Is it mornin'?" she asks quietly.

"Almost," I tell her. "Do you remember how your Nana had daydreams?" She nods. "I have night dreams. But they are more than dreams sometimes. Sometimes they tell me something that I need to do. Does that make sense?"

Juni sits up further and reaches her hand out to touch my temple—right where I felt the burn earlier.

"Pretty," she says. She begins tracing shapes along my temples, looking at something in awe. I walk over to the small, mirrored glass that sits by the bathtub. That is when I see silvery tattoos on my face. They look like different moon phases.

"Do you know what this means?" I ask Juni.

"Magic," she replies.

I am running out of time. If my plan is going to work, I need to leave before the sun rises. "I had a vision, Juni. I need you to be a brave girl for me, okay?"

"What do you mean?"

"I need to leave for a little while. The vision told me what I need to do to keep you safe. You must stay with Sylas, okay? I will come back for you. I promise. I have seen it in my magical dream. Just like your Nana. Okay?"

Juni's lips begin to quiver, and her teary eyes match my own.

"I love you, Juni. I promise that you will be safe with Sylas. I will come back for you as soon as I can." I pull her into my arms and hold her as we both cry.

"You promise you will come back?"

"I promise, honey. You are mine. I will come back for you."

I quickly pack a small bag for myself and then scoop Juni back into my arms, sneaking out of our tent and over to Sylas's home. I need to get her safely inside before I leave.

"Sylas," I whisper. His home is different from the one that we stayed in. It has a main living space with separate rooms for bedrooms. He meets us in the living area.

When he sees us crying, he immediately goes on alert. "What is wrong? Did something happen?" He checks us both over, looking for injuries.

"Not yet. I do not have much time. I have visions. Like what Juni's Nana had. I had one tonight and I need to leave the outpost before the sun rises. It is the only way to keep Juni safe." I cannot share many details of what I must do so I keep it vague. "I need you to protect Juni for me for a little while. I will be back as soon as it is safe. Can you do that?"

"Of course," he replies. "I will always keep her safe. But will *you* be okay? I can protect you too."

"I have seen what happens. This is the only way. I will be back for her. She is mine and I would not leave her if there was another way."

"I understand. I promise I will take care of her. We will be here waiting for you to return."

"Please don' go, Reese. Sylas will protect you too. I am strong. I will protect you." Juni cries as she begs me to stay.

"I must go, sweetie. It is the only way. I will be back when the air is warm. I saw it in my vision. Be brave for me, okay?" I wrap my arms tightly around her little body. "I love you."

"I love you too, Reese. I will be brave."

I pass Juni over to Sylas as she cries and tries to cling to me. "You cannot trust Zuri with her," I tell him as I head for the door. He nods his understanding and holds Juni to his chest as she cries out for me.

With tears soaking my cheeks, I leave the outpost and head west—right into the trap that Zuri set for me.

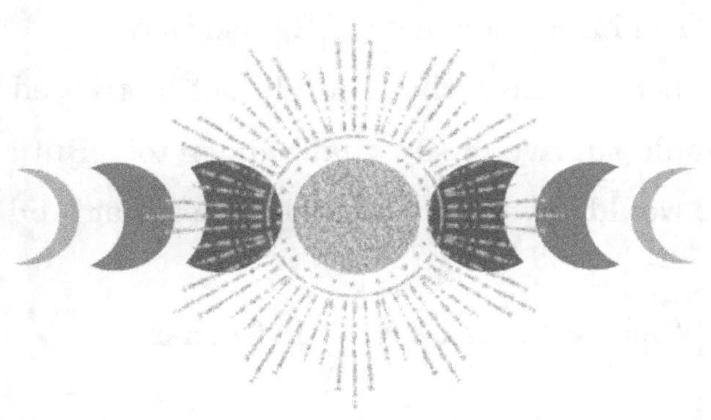

Chapter Four

Reese

(Present Day)

"So, you got caught on purpose?" Ro asks me. "Why on Earth would you do that? You had to know that she was going to do something awful to you."

I knew exactly what would be done to me. "Yes. It was what my vision had told me to do. If I stayed at the outpost with Juni, Zuri would have led Dreena's pack right to us. Juni, Sylas, Jasper, Fiske, Zya, and I would have all died in the attack. Zuri would have died too—which may have been a good thing considering what she did here—but it was too much to risk. It was the only way."

"You lured them away," Ramsey says.

I nod. "I knew that I would not be treated kindly, but I would survive. I saw that happen too. But even if I didn't, I would have still made the choice that I did to save Juni."

"What happened next?" Griffin asks.

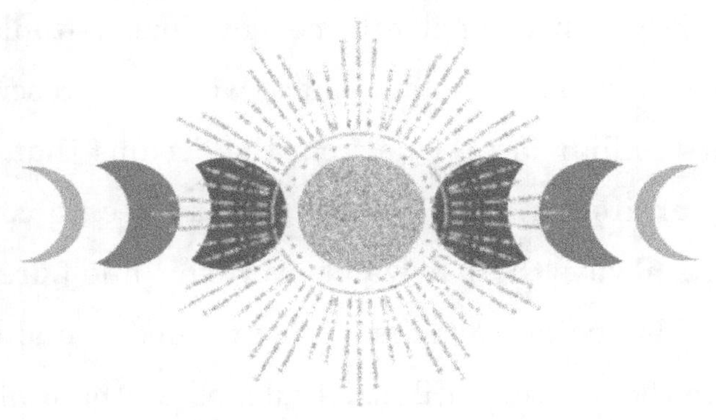

Chapter Five

(Dreena's Encampment)

Zuri handed me over to Dreena's band of witch hunters. We traveled for days, maybe weeks. I had no real way of keeping track. My hands and feet were tied, and I was blindfolded. The constant jostling of the sled that I was pulled in exasperated my already aching head. They did not offer me any food, though I was given water a few times each day. I vomited it all up. By the time we arrived at my new temporary home, I was already weak and barely able to stay awake.

My vision did not tell me how long I would be a prisoner here—but I knew that I would be rescued by another familiar face. One from the dreams that I have had my entire life. My Viking. He had been a constant presence, always there to watch over me while I dreamt of new worlds and adventures. I just needed to endure the pain and the hunger until he found me. But he *would* find me. I had to believe that his role in my vision was accurate and not just the imaginary presence that appeared in all of my dreams.

My head hurt so badly that I couldn't keep anything down. My wrists are bloody from being tied up. I was beaten daily. Kicked, hit, spit on. My ribs feel broken, and I know that my face was swollen. I was given dirty water to drink. But I held onto hope. I trusted my vision. He *would* find me. My Viking. Taller than any man I had ever met, blond hair, shaved on the sides and braided down the middle. Layer after layer of muscle. Eyes so blue, it felt like I was sinking into the ocean as I looked at them. He *would* find me. He had to.

I lost track of time. Every day since I allowed myself to be captured by Zuri, I was told that it would be my last—but the next day always came. Like me, they were waiting for something. But I am not sure what.

After it was clear that I was too weak and sick to be any kind of threat, the witch hunters left me alone. The periods of time when I was awake, I would listen—spy. Try to gather as much information as I could while I sat helplessly in a pile of my own filth. It started mostly out of boredom, but I also knew that any information that I could learn might be helpful one day.

I learned that I was back in Nightfury, though not under the control of the Nightfury Alpha. They were squatters. Hiding in plain sight. This was a new home for them—having left the other territories to come together here.

The night before I was rescued, the snippets of information started to all come together.

A wolf named Dreena started this witch hunt. She was the face of the rebellion. But to me, it was clear that she was a pawn. A tool for another wolf to rise to power.

Briggs.

Briggs is the brother of the Beta for Nightfury. He felt slighted that he was not chosen as Beta. He always felt jealous of his brother, Boone. Briggs, a soldier, seduced Dreena. He made her believe that he loved her. He told her that they were True Mates, but her wolf could not feel it because of a curse that the witches placed on her. He took her to bed and then whispered into her ear each night. It did not take long before he had hijacked her rebellion for his own benefit.

Dreena became paranoid. Her mind fractured. She started taking medicines and elixirs to try and rid her body of the curse. Briggs encouraged her, poisoning her mind as well as her body. He convinced her that the only way to break the curse was to kill the witches.

Briggs knew that if Dreena was killed, her supporters would transfer over to him. He planned to build his own pack—one that would rival the others.

Briggs convinced Dreena that it would be best to kill me the next day. It would be a full moon, and she believed that if I was killed during the moon, my powers would transfer over to them. But that is not what Briggs had planned at all.

Briggs was going to kill Dreena and then force a bond with me under the full moon. It was the only real way to share powers. If I was bonded to him, he would gain my magic. It would make him stronger, and he would use me as a shield against my sisters and their Alphas.

I knew that he would not be successful. My Viking would save me in time. But that did not stop the panic I felt when Briggs paid me a visit, letting me know all of the disgusting ways he planned to use my body while he stole my magic.

What if the vision changed? I know that leaving Juni with Sylas and luring Zuri away from the outpost was the only way to save them—but so much time has passed since then. Is it possible that my fate has changed since then?

I made up my mind that night. If my Viking did not come for me before Briggs did, I would cut my own throat. Vision be damned.

So that night, while everyone drank and banged and celebrated my upcoming murder, I waited. Alert. Ready to make my move.

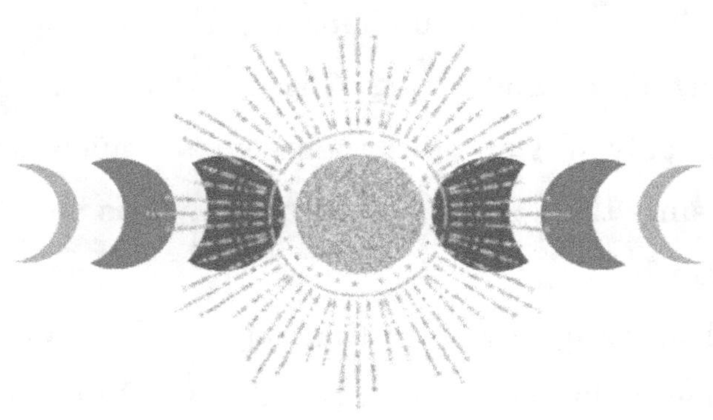

Chapter Six

(Dreena's Encampment)

I received word that Dreena and her followers had made camp in one of my abandoned outposts. The base had already been stripped of weapons and supplies, but the structures still stood. I used to keep a team of soldiers at the camp, but it has sat empty for the last 20 years or so.

Strategically, it is a smart place for Dreena to set up. The bones were already there–she just needed to fill it with bodies and supplies. What is most concerning to me, however, is that Dreena should not know that this base exists. Her followers are from Nightfang and

Nighthowl. They are not soldiers who have access to maps of our bases.

It could only mean one thing. Dreena has help.

Over the last several days since I arrived, the camp has been flooded with wolves. Over 200 by my count. I stay hidden as I wait for backup. Dreena is in there somewhere. I have seen glimpses of her. If there were only 50, I might risk a stealthy incursion with only my Beta as backup. But I cannot take on 200 wolves by myself. With every new group that makes it to the encampment, I look for children. So far, there have been none which will make the impending bloodshed easier to swallow.

Sleds with supplies are brought into the camp every few days. Probably goods that have been stolen from outposts in the other territories.

Scanning the sleds with my thermal vision as they arrive shows nothing of great concern being brought to the camp. Food, furs, tools, and weapons. All things that I would suspect. I would sabotage their shipments but that would tip them off to my presence, and I am not ready for that yet. I keep track of anyone entering or leaving the camp. For the most part, nobody leaves unless it is to meet a shipment.

One day, while scanning a sled, my vision picks up on an abnormal heat signature. It is possible that the sled contains a recent kill, but when it is not brought over to the canteen to be processed, my hackles raise. The heat signature is too small to be a wolf. Could they have a child? If so, it would be the first one that I have noticed.

Trusting my gut, I know that it is something that I need to investigate further. If pups were beginning to arrive, I would need to attack before my team has fully assembled. If it is something else, I need to know that too.

Focusing my attention on that part of the camp, I wait. Hours later, Dreena emerges from one of the buildings in that area. This time, she is not alone. Walking next to her, I find my traitor.

Briggs.

Boone's brother.

"I have eyes on Dreena. Your brother is with her. He is our traitor."

His reply is instant. *"Fucking Briggs."*

Briggs being here does not at all make me question Boone's loyalty to me. Briggs has always been jealous of his brother. He could have made a strong Beta if he did not have such a thirst for power. He stole it without any hesitation or remorse, even if that meant hurting others in the process. He has been a constant thorn in my side, always stirring up shit wherever he is stationed.

*"You will need to be extra cautious when you get into range. He needs to be taken care of,"*I tell Boone.

"I will take him down myself, Alpha."

"If it comes to it. There is possibly a child being held at the camp. I do not have eyes on them, but the heat signature is too small for an adult."

"Noted. We will proceed with caution. When will the rest of our backup be here? We cannot just keep watching."

"By the full moon. Dreena keeps to the center of the camp. We will go in and remove her, hopefully without causing too much alarm. They drink and fuck in excess nightly. We need to use that to our advantage."

"Have you updated your brothers?"

"Not yet. The headaches are too bad. I do not want to lose focus."

*"I will send an update when I am able,"*he tells me.

Communicating mind to mind with my brothers, like I can with Boone and other pack members, affects me a little differently. It causes headaches that can be distracting at best and debilitating at worst. We are not sure why, exactly, but it is a skill that did not present itself as an option until we all became Alphas. It is not something that all siblings can do—I actually do not know of any other siblings who can, other than those who have a relationship as Alpha and Beta, like my father had with his brother before he died. When I am on a mission, I limit my communication so that I do not suffer any lapse in focus—though it is still a valuable asset that we utilize when necessary.

My last update I provided to my brothers was when I first arrived. I told them that I would remain on lookout, staying at a great enough distance so that my presence would not be noticed by the enemy wolves, until my team arrived. Not wanting to draw attention, I chose wolves from different outposts, spread across the territory for this mission. Because of that, it will take some time for everyone to get into position.

The headache caused by my last communication with my brothers burned across my temples. It was unlike anything that I have ever felt before.

Movement in the camp pulls me out of my thoughts. I cannot get a clear visual on that heat signature, but it is still hot. Still living. But it's hardly moving. My wolf is restless, itching to get inside the camp. It is so fucking tempting to sneak in alone. My fixation on that heat signature is distracting but I cannot pull my eyes away.

Later that week, my task force arrives. We discuss strategy, our informants telling us that there is something happening the night of the full moon, but the celebration has clearly started early. Drunken shouts and carnal moans are our cue that this is the moment to strike. We know that we will only get one shot like this, and we need to take it.

On my command, a line of my soldiers circle the outpost while another group followed me in. I lead my wolves through the camp, using the buildings as cover. Any of the wolves that we encounter are too drunk or distracted to think that we are their enemy. They have become too comfortable, and it works in our favor.

Following the plan, I lead my wolves on a path that will bring us straight to Dreena's lodging. I watched her go inside with Briggs not long ago–they will be distracted. But I cannot make myself stay on course. I have an uncontrollable *need* to find out what that mysterious heat signature is.

"Boone, take the lead. Capture if you can. Kill if you must."

Nobody questions the change in plan, and I know that I can trust Boone to lead the team. Ideally, we would capture Dreena and Briggs to hold a public trial and execution or banishment. It would be the most effective way to show their supporters that they have lost. But, if they meet their end here tonight, I will not be mad about it. They have caused too many issues for my brothers and their Mates for me to feel any guilt in ending their lives here.

I separate from my group, weaving around drunk partiers, walking past a female getting absolutely railed by two males. They are too lost in lust to notice the massive Alpha walking by.

After a few strategic maneuvers to keep myself hidden, I found her. The heat signature. Not a child or a wolf, but a human with pale skin, fiery hair, and angry green eyes. The third sister. Reese. My Mate.

Her wild, fiery hair shines bright in the moonlight. The beauty of the copper shade stands in contrast to the dank conditions surrounding her. Her deep green eyes divert my gaze as the flecks of gold within them glitter in time with the crackling fire. She is enchanting. A beauty that I have only ever seen in my dreams.

I am captivated.

Reese is small–smaller than Rowan by an inch or two. She is filthy—only skin and bones. The scent of bile surrounds her where she is curled up on the ground. She will need proper nutrition, rest, healing for the open wounds I can see and scent.

Even in her disheveled state, she is alluring.

She notices me as I slink closer, not wanting to draw too much attention but unable to hold myself back to come up with a plan. My wolf is insistent that we need to take her, keep her safe. He no longer cares about the mission as all his focus is on her.

My Mate.

Before I can reach her, all hell breaks loose in the camp. Chaos surrounds me as I close the remaining distance between us—no longer caring who might see. Reese is still curled up on her side, but her eyes have shuttered closed. She holds her head and whimpers. The noise of the attack does not force her eyes to open—the fight is rapidly getting closer to us. I should turn around and fight with my soldiers. I should make sure that Dreena and Briggs are secured. But instead, I shift. I pull at the shackles until they break, freeing Reese from the heavy chains that kept her immobile. She weighs nothing as I lift her into my arms.

Despite the battle being waged all around me, I walk through the fray, snarling at anyone who tries to stand in my way. I do not want a Mate, I cannot have one, but I will not let anyone else fucking touch her again.

Her hair falls from her face, giving me the first glimpse of her moon markings. Silvery moons adorn her

49

temples. Seeing them, I know that I must have the same markings. The burning headache that I felt weeks ago—this must have been what caused it. It would not have been visible to anyone while in my wolf form.

I walk with Reese cradled in my arms until we are a safe distance away from the outpost. She is unconscious, either asleep or passed out. Based on how thin she is, it appears that she has not eaten in weeks. The shirt that she wears is in tatters, covered in blood, dirt, and vomit. Her wrists and ankles are bloody from the chains. Bruising around her ribs tells me that they are probably broken as well. She has bruises on her face and legs too. They must have beaten her in addition to starving her. I cannot tell how old the wounds are—I know that humans heal slower than shifters—but if she was beaten while I sat nearby waiting to act, I am not sure I would ever forgive myself.

Removing the shreds of her clothing, I carefully wipe away some of the grime with water from my canteen. That is when I smell it. Infection. I cannot see a festering wound, but the smell is unmistakable.

I need a plan.

"We have a problem, Alpha." Boone's frustrated message cuts through my thoughts. *"Dreena and Briggs*

escaped.   We followed their scent.   They crossed the border.”

Fuck! If they crossed the border, we would have to wait them out to see if they return. I will not risk sending my wolves into bear territory.

“We will add more patrols to the borders. If they step foot back into our territory, they will be killed on sight. Any other updates?”

“About 30 surrendered. 100 or so fled. About 60 dead. No casualties from our side.”

“Detain those who surrendered and move them to Ire Outpost. I will be traveling to Tempest with the human that I rescued. She needs medical attention.”

“Human? One of the sisters?”

“I believe so.”

I do not tell him that she is my Mate. I do not tell anyone. I do not even want to admit it to myself. Because I do not want a Mate.

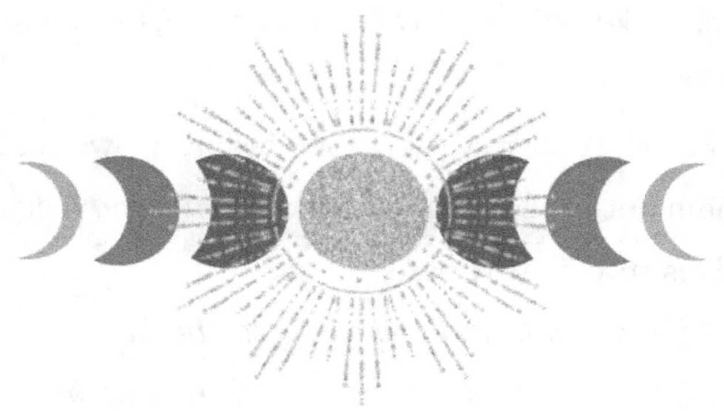

Chapter Seven

(Tempest Outpost)

One week ago, I woke up in a large bed that smelled of cedar and vanilla tobacco. There was a fire burning in the hearth, but I was alone. I tried to sit up but as I was nearly to my feet, a stern looking woman entered the room and made me lay back down. She fussed over me, applying ointments to my wounds and checking me for a fever, and then left.

I later learned that this woman's name is Clara, and she was the healer at Tempest Outpost. From what she told me, the Nightfury Alpha brought me here after I was found nearly dead at the witch hunter's encampment. I was given strict orders to eat, hydrate, and rest. I am not allowed to leave this room. Apparently, I was moved from one prison to another. At least this one has indoor plumbing.

In the time that I have been here, I have not met anyone else. My injuries are slowly healing, and my headaches are getting better. With a steady supply of nourishing foods, I am feeling stronger.

I dream about Juniper and miss her every day. I also dream about my Viking. In my vision, I was rescued by my mystery dream man. But in reality, I'm not sure what happened. I have to believe that my vision was accurate, and I will see Juni again. She needs to be okay.

After another day of being sequestered in my room, I toss and turn in my sleep. I feel so restless, if I do not leave this room, I am going to go insane. Quietly sneaking out of bed, I slowly pull open the door that leads to some sort of hallway. I am so focused on making sure that nobody is guarding the hall that I do not notice the large golden wolf that is asleep at my feet and I trip over him, screeching as I tumble. Strong hands reach out to help me and I come face to face with the man of my dreams.

"What are you doing?" he grumbles. His voice is low, growly, and exactly like I imagined it would be.

My eyes make a quick, involuntary glance down before I realize that he is naked. I keep my eyes trained on his face and refuse to look again.

"Honestly, I think I was looking for you, maybe." My confession does not come out as confident as I would have liked, but I am completely distracted by his striking blue eyes. They are even more vivid than I was ever able to conjure up in my dreams. Getting lost in them for a few moments more, I feel something settle within my chest. I'm immediately put at ease and the itchy feeling that I was starting to feel being trapped alone in that room for over a week completely falls away. "Are you okay? I didn't mean to trip over you."

His eyes scan my body, and I feel my cheeks heat, knowing that I am only wearing an oversized shirt. "You should be in bed," he growls.

Okay... Apparently, the beast-like gruffness is an all the time thing.

"All that I have done since I came here is rest. I need to see something other than the same four walls before I pull my hair out."

His hand reaches towards me as he checks my hair, making sure that I haven't actually pulled any out.

I snort. "It's just an expression," I explain. "I am going stir crazy."

"So, you came to find me?"

"Well, yeah." I laugh. "I'm sorry. I just realized that I do not actually know who you are. You have been in my dreams since I was a little girl, so it kind of feels like I know you."

"In your dreams?" He is looking at me like I am crazy. Which, fair. I'm not sure that I am totally sane myself since I was magically transported to a world of shifters where my dreams are reality.

"Yep. Apparently, I have magical dreams. Visions, I guess. But since the world that I came from didn't have any magic, I didn't know that my dreams were more than that until I woke up here." I shrug. "Every dream that I have had, for as long as I can remember, has had you in them. Always. No matter what the dream was about. Several weeks ago, I had a vision that you would find me at that camp but then I couldn't stay awake long enough to see if it actually happened."

I reach up to touch the moon markings on his face. He flinches away from my touch as if I burned him. I immediately pull my hand back.

"Sorry. Those are new. You never had the markings in my dreams," I explain.

"You have them too." His words are now only about 80% growl as he points at the markings on my temples. Progress.

"I know. They are new for me too. Do you know what they mean? They must mean something. Magic, I suppose. But it has to be more than that, right? Why would we both have them?"

He sighs, clearly not wanting to have this conversation with me at all. But he does answer. "They are Moon Touched markings. They mean that The Moon granted you additional magic. It is rare."

Moon magic? "But I don't have any magic at all. Other than my dreams, which I suppose are probably magic. But I didn't know that they were real until recently. Is that what it means?" I look up into his eyes. Does he feel this innate comfort in my presence like I do with him?

"Maybe." Short. To the point. Not at all helpful.

I try a different approach. "Why do *you* have them?"

He turns and starts walking away from me. "Go back to bed, Wildflower."

And that's how he left me. His perfect ass retreating further into the dark hallway as I stood shocked still–with more questions than I had before this lovely little chat happened.

I sink down and sit against the door. The floor is still warm from where his wolf slept not long ago. I cannot go back into that room right now. Since I have nothing better to do, I look around the hall. This building looks more permanent than the structures that I saw in Nightfang and at the encampment. The walls are made of stone and wood instead of leather and fabric. The spot where I sit smells strongly of the same cedar and vanilla tobacco that the inside of the room smells like. Is it him? Am I staying in his room and is that why he was sleeping out in the hall? There must be another place for me to stay that doesn't force him out of his bed. Especially since he clearly does not want me here.

I stand up and walk down the hallway, opening the next door that I see, and peeking inside. This room is smaller but appears to be unoccupied. It does not smell like him. It does not smell like anything, really. Risking a potentially awkward Goldilocks moment, I make the decision to use this room instead. I would much rather slum it with Cranky Clara than stay where I am not welcome.

Crawling into this new, cold bed, I turn away from the door and refuse to cry. Clearly, I misread the importance of my Viking showing up in my dreams and then his rescuing me from the witch hunters. I was so excited to meet him, and he wants nothing to do with me. It is hard to not let the disappointment sink in.

I don't even know his name.

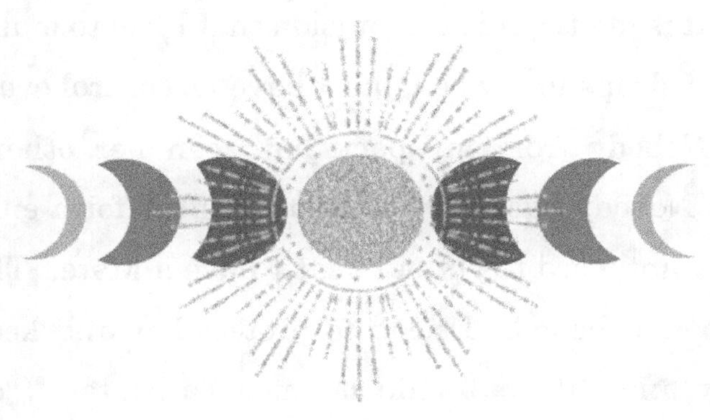

Chapter Eight

It is getting harder to keep my distance from my Mate. We are staying in my lodge at Tempest outpost—a home that I built for myself as soon as I was old enough to leave our family's lodge. I have always felt at peace here, but I have not had a decent night's sleep since we arrived. I could blame it on the fact that she has taken over my private rooms and commandeered my bed.

But, ever since that night that she tripped over me in the hallway, she has put herself to bed in the spare room.

And every night, I move her back to my bed after she falls asleep.

It is idiotic, this compulsion that I feel to make sure that she sleeps in my bed, but I have no control over it.

Nobody from my pack has seen her other than Clara. Nobody has seen me in my shifted form either. I do not want word to get out that I have a Mate. That we are Moon Touched. I need to protect her and keep her healthy and safe—but I do not need a Mate. I cannot handle the distraction or the absolute despair that will happen when I lose her.

After I cleared everyone other than Clara out of Tempest lodge, I told Clara that she could give Reese a tour of the building. It is much smaller than our family lodge in the main village, but there are still other rooms to explore. We have a small library—though she will not be able to read any of the books—and the kitchen is available for her to get a snack anytime she likes. I lock myself in my office during the day so that we do not cross paths. At night, I wait for her to fall asleep and then I move her to my room and sleep outside the door.

It is fucked. But it is where we are at right now.

I know that if she sees me, she will continue to ask questions that I do not want to answer. How do I tell her that she holds the other half of my soul, but I refuse to allow myself to love her? How do I explain that there is no possible way for her to choose another—yet I cannot be the one for her either?

She is so fucking young.

So fucking beautiful.

But I cannot go there. I saw how it ended for my father—how his heart shattered into a million pieces, and he never recovered. He was no longer able to be Alpha. He could not even find the strength to raise us. Our eyes haunted him. My coloring—my wolf—haunted him. I would not survive a loss like that.

So, I avoid her. I move her to my bed, give her my shirts to wear, and make sure that she is fed because it soothes my wolf. But I cannot love her.

Looking outside, I decide that it is late enough to go through our nightly routine. She is always asleep by now. She sleeps so soundly that she has never woken up while I move her back down the hall.

When I open the door to the spare room, I find it empty. I go to my room, ignoring the flutters in my stomach, thinking that she might have chosen my room instead, but that room is empty too. Panic begins to set in. She has to be here somewhere.

I race to the kitchen, hoping that she went looking for a late-night snack. Empty.

The main living space. Empty.

I open the door to the library. Initially, I found it empty as well. But then I hear a small noise. A sniffle. Is she crying?

Looking closer at the room, I find Reese curled up in a dark corner. She is holding her head and crying. I rush over and crouch down beside her.

"Reese? Are you okay?" I keep my voice as soft as possible, not wanting to frighten her.

"Beast?" I hold back a chuckle at the nickname she has given me. Clara told me that Reese refers to me as The Beast, but since I have been avoiding her, she has not said it to my face. Her voice is so small, so delicate. I do not want to do anything that might break her.

"What is going on? Why are you crying?" I look her over, trying to find any injury or reason for her to be upset. Did she fall?

"You can just go. You don't have to pretend to care."

Her voice sounds so defeated as she curls into herself even more on the floor. I have to stop a whimper before it leaves my chest. "Please tell me."

Letting out a sigh, she makes eye contact with me before speaking again. "My head hurts. I miss my sisters. My period started. I need to get back to Juni. I'm stuck in a house with a grump who avoids me. I am clearly not welcome here. And to top it all off, I don't even know your name! Did I say that my head hurts? Because my head really, really hurts."

As she lists her many complaints, I feel my guts twist. My Wildflower is hurting, and I did not even know because I have kept my distance.

"Did Clara leave you any medicine for the headaches? She thought that they would go away now that your infection has passed."

"It doesn't help. I told her that, but she didn't listen." Reese's lip quivers as she tries to calm herself down to explain. "They aren't regular headaches. I was diagnosed with chronic migraines back in my world. I was on a prescribed medication, but I did not have any with me when I was transported here. The headaches make my head hurt so bad that I get dizzy and throw up."

I cannot stop my whimper this time. Has she been suffering this entire time? Clara told me that the medicine would help. I should have made sure.

"What can I do to help?"

"I don't know," she sighs. "Bright lights make it worse. My period makes it worse. Stress makes it worse."

I try to help her sit up, propping her against the bookcase. "What is a period? You have said that word a couple of times, but I do not understand what that is."

"Oh. Um. My menstrual cycle. Is that a thing here? I'm afraid my extensive education on wolf shifters did not cover reproductive cycles." She presses the heels of her hands to her eyes. "I'm bleeding."

Bleeding? "You are hurt? Where?" I reach for her, wanting to see if it is something that I can heal for her.

"Not that kind of bleeding. I mean, I don't have a wound. It is just part of being a human. A woman. I bleed each month as part of my reproductive cycle. Wolves have heats, right? Humans don't have that. It's different for us. Don't worry about it. I shouldn't have said anything. I will just deal." Her cheeks heat and she looks away. She is embarrassed.

I do not want her to have to 'just deal'. I need to provide for her. I should have been making sure that she is okay.

"Can I help you back to your room? You will be more comfortable there than on the floor. Why are you on the floor, anyway?"

She lets me help her up. It is then that I notice the blood on the shirt she is wearing. I make the decision to figure out how to help her with her period later. First, I will get her cleaned up and tucked into bed. She wobbles as she stands. Dizzy. How could I let her go through all of this alone? What is wrong with me?

She laughs, though it sounds more like a groan. "I was bored so I decided that I would try to find a book to read. But I can't read this language, so I thought that maybe there were books with pictures in them or something. I was trying to reach a book on one of the taller shelves, but I got dizzy and fell. I'm okay. It was just best that I stayed down there until the dizziness and waves of nausea passed. Moving just makes it worse."

She would have stayed on the floor all night if I had not found her.

"I have met Rowan," I tell her. Hoping that her sister is a safe topic for us to talk about as we make our way back to my room. "I know that Ramsey is safe as well. She arrived at the lodge after I was last there."

Excitement and hope fill her eyes. "Will you take me to them?"

"Of course. Once it is safe to travel."

"We need to pick Juni up first, though. I promised her."

"Who is Juni?"

"She is a little girl. About 4 years old. She is safe with her True Mate right now, but I am her guardian. It is kind of a long story, but I had to leave her at the outpost with her True Mate to protect her. But my vision showed me that we will pick her up on our way home. Once the weather is warm."

She has a daughter? Is she human like Reese or is she from this world? Rowan did not say anything about her sister having a child. They must have met in this world.

"How did you meet her?"

Once we get into the room, I pull her through to the bathroom and begin filling up the bathtub.

"She found me." Her words are soft, slightly pained from her headache. But she continues. "When I first arrived in this world, I had almost frozen to death. I woke up in the middle of a snowy forest. I had a migraine so bad that I could not open my eyes, but I stumbled around until I found a small cave. When I woke up again, a little bear cub was curled up next to me, keeping me warm. When she shifted into her human form, I realized that she was the same little girl that is always in my dreams. Just like you."

"You have said that before. That I was in your dreams. What do you mean?"

"I do not know why, but ever since I was a little girl, I have always had very vivid dreams. Ramsey always told me that it is because I had an active imagination, but now I am wondering if it is because of this moon magic that I apparently have." She taps gently on her temple. "Either way, there were faces that always showed up in my dreams. Well, some of them showed up only sometimes but there were two faces that were always there. Juniper…and you. I don't know what it means but I do know that Juni's heart string led her to me and then to her True Mate. Mine led me to you."

She feels it too. The pull of our souls.

I add some relaxing salts and oils into the bathwater and then place a towel and fresh shirt on the vanity.

"Do you need help in the bath? I can call for Clara if it makes you feel more comfortable."

She looks around the room, only now noticing that I have prepared a bath for her. "Oh. Um. I will be okay. Will you leave the door cracked open, though? Just in case?"

"Of course. I will be right outside. Let me know if you need anything."

I am still so frustrated with myself that I have done such a great job at fucking this all up. I do not know anything about humans. Rowan was already bonded to War when I met her. Her body had already changed. Hell, she was already pregnant. I do not have any women's clothing here. I could borrow something from Clara, but it would not fit her any better than my shirts do. She is so much smaller than shifter females.

She is bleeding, but not from an injury. I am not sure how to help her with that. I doubt Clara will know what to do and I do not think that my saliva will heal her.

Fuck. The thought of licking her cunt has made me painfully hard. It has been too long since I have had a good fuck. And now it will not ever happen unless I can convince Reese into agreeing to a physical relationship. No feelings. No love. Maybe she will go for it. Rowan seems to be sexually open. Maybe Reese is too?

It does not matter. Now is not the time for that discussion anyway. I will just take care of myself again later tonight.

I find the tea that helps with head pain. It is the same tea that I drink regularly. There is another that will help her sleep, if she wants to take it.

I quickly head to the kitchen for a clean cup and some hot water before returning to my room. Reese is coming out of the bathroom dressed in a fresh shirt and squeezing some of the water out of her hair with the towel as I walk in.

"I think that we should try some of the tea for your headache. It is the strongest pain relief that I have here.

I also have a blend that will help you sleep–if that is something that you want."

"I will try both," she tells me, sounding defeated. "Are you sure that you want me to sleep in here? I feel bad taking your bed. And, without menstrual products or even underwear, I am going to bleed all over your sheets."

"You do not need to worry about that. I just want you to feel better and get some rest."

"I could do that in the other room. Why do you keep bringing me back to your room when it is clear that you do not want me here?"

A low growl rumbles from my chest. My wolf does not like that she feels unwanted.

"It is not that I do not want you here," I explain. "I just do not know what I am doing. I did not expect to find my Mate." As soon as the words are out of my mouth, I feel the need to take them back. I have avoided her questions about us being Mates. Now I have just confirmed it.

"It's true, then? We are Heart Mates? Or, True Mates, right? That is what wolves call it? Is that the pull that I feel? It is our souls finding each other? Is that what we have matching moon marks?"

Fuck. "Yes."

"Well, what does that mean for us?" Reese's words hold more than just a question.

My wolf scratches to get out—to stop me from hurting my Mate with my words. But I do it anyway. "Nothing," I say sharply. "I cannot have a Mate."

I see the hope that had filled her eyes instantly deflate. She rears back as if I slapped her. I might as well have.

My wolf roars at me as I walk out of the room, leaving my Mate and her hopes behind.

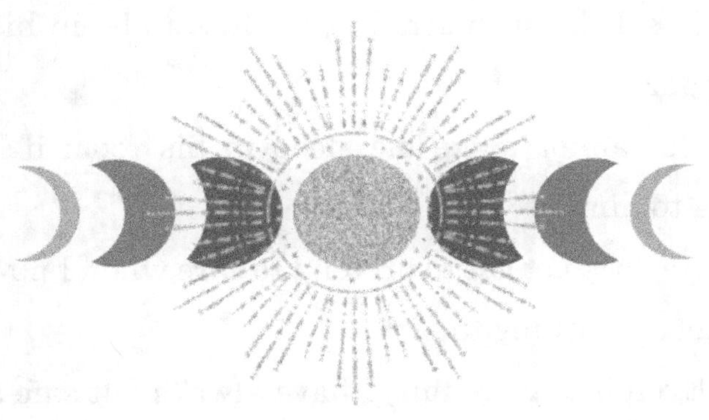

Chapter Nine

Reese

I keep replaying his words in my mind. *Nothing. I cannot have a Mate. What does that mean for us? Nothing.*

What do I mean to you? Nothing–that is what he meant.

It means nothing? This feeling in my chest that tells me I have found the person I am meant to be with– that I share my literal soul with–and it means *nothing*?

I wait until I hear the click of his office door before I leave his room and go to the room down the hall. Once inside, I lock the door. Then, I push the desk that sits in the corner of the room up against it. I add all of the furniture that I can move to the barricade. I do not know

71

where I find the strength, but I refuse to be in his space any longer.

He cannot make me sleep in his room if I mean nothing to him.

He does not get to pretend to care when I now know that I mean nothing to him.

Even in my dreams, I have always felt safe around him. But his words have hurt worse than any blade. *Nothing.*

What a way to kick a girl when she is already down.

I will leave in the morning. If he will not take me to Juni and my sisters, then I will find someone who will. They are the only ones who have ever wanted me anyway.

I will not be his problem any longer.

In reality, it takes three days before I am able to pull myself out of bed. Without medication, my migraine lasted the entirety of my period, and I didn't have the energy to force another conversation with the grump.

He did not try to move me that first night that I was barricaded in my room. Truthfully, I don't even think that he noticed that I had moved.

On the second night, he pounded on the door and told me to remove the barricade. He again might not have noticed that I was in the spare room, but Cranky Clara ratted me out. The loud bangs on the door exasperated my headache and I barely got to the toilet in time to puke up the non-existent food in my belly. I made a mental note to stock up on snacks next time before I lock myself away in a room.

On the third night, he pleaded with me through the door to move the barricade, even if I did it just long enough so that Clara could bring in some medicine and food. I ignored him—refused to even give him proof of life, though he could probably hear me through the door. That is when he scared the shit out of me as he broke in through the window.

Not saying a word, he unblocked my door and then left. Clara was sent in with a tray of food and some tea, but I didn't touch it.

Am I being childish? Probably. Do I care? Not one bit. I am heartbroken. I am lonely. I am pissed off. I still do not even know his name. I probably haven't earned the right to know it since I am *nothing*, after all.

When I do finally emerge from my room early the next morning, I am wrapped in nothing but a blanket. The shirt that I had been wearing was stained and dirty. I did not want to put it back on after my bath. I step around my guard dog's body and head straight to his room, pulling a fresh shirt from his wardrobe and slipping it over my head.

I find a small leather bag and stuff another shirt inside before heading to the kitchen for the rest of my travel necessities.

He enters the kitchen while pulling on some pants.

"What the fuck do you think you are doing?" he growls at me.

I raise my eyebrows in response.

He takes a deep breath and then tries again. "Are you leaving?"

"Yes. I am going to go and find my child. Then I will find my sisters."

"By yourself?"

"If I must. I know that I do not mean anything to you, but they mean the world to me. I have spent my entire life being passed around from one home to another, never being someone's first choice. The only people who have ever chosen me are my sisters and Juni. I'm sorry that you got stuck with me as a Mate, but I refuse to stay in a situation when I am not wanted."

I cannot keep the tremor out of my voice or the tears from falling, but I stand tall. When he doesn't say anything, I finish packing my bag and skirt around him to leave the kitchen.

"Well, I guess this is goodbye then...whatever your name is. Please thank Clara for her care."

It is my turn to walk away. Leave him standing alone in the room.

A loud growl comes out of the kitchen. "Reese, wait," his voice follows me down the hall, but I keep walking. "Fuck. Please. Please wait."

He catches up to me and gently reaches for my arm. I wait for him to speak but when nothing comes out of his mouth, I scoff, rip my arm free, and turn away again.

"Can you at least point me in the direction of Nightfang?" I ask as I gesture wildly out into the world.

"Bade," he grunts.

"What?"

He closes his eyes, his shoulder slumping. "Bade. My name is Bade. I am sorry that I am fucking this all up. None of this is supposed to be this way."

"Whether it is supposed to be this way or not, this is the way that it is. You have made it clear that you do not want a Mate and all that I have ever wanted is to be wanted. Do you understand how crushing that is for me? How gutted I felt when you told me that us being True Mates meant nothing? I cannot stay here, with you, in your home and be ignored. Neglected."

"I made sure you were taken care of."

"You didn't even tell me your name until two seconds ago! I have been here for weeks! Emotional needs are just as important as physical ones."

"I cannot give you more."

"Then I don't know what else to tell you. I guess I will see you around." I walk out into the outpost. People and wolves stop and stare as I pass, whispering behind my back as I head for the gate. This is my first time outside since I arrived. I didn't even know that all of this was out here. Maybe one of the soldiers at the gate can point me in the right direction.

"Hello, gentlemen," I greet as I get closer, "you wouldn't happen to have a map, would you? I need to get to Nightfang."

"I'm sorry, miss, but we are not authorized to let you leave," the younger of the two guards states.

"Are you fucking kidding me right now?" I shout, unable to control my anger.

"The order came directly from the Alpha." The tips of his ears turn pink as he looks down at his feet.

"I bet it did," I scoff. "You can tell your Alpha that he can shove his order right up his ass." I push past the guards and leave the outpost.

Less than ten minutes later, a large golden wolf catches up to me. He loops around to face me before he shifts.

"I will go with you, but it will take weeks if you insist on walking." His words are more growl than anything.

I scoff. "How else will I get there? Is there a train or a plane that I missed?"

"You can ride on my back."

I cackle at the suggestion. "No thanks."

"It will cut our travel time in half, if not more."

I bite my lip as I think through my options. Riding on his back will allow us to travel faster, but it would mean trusting him enough to not drop me. And it would mean straddling him while going commando in nothing but an oversized shirt. The sooner I get Juni, the sooner I can find my sisters, the sooner I can move on.

"Fine. But if you drop me and I die, I will haunt you for the rest of your ridiculously long life."

Bade nods once and then shifts back into his wolf. He lowers down to his belly so that I can climb on and then he takes off. I squeal and pull his fur, trying to stay on. Apparently, I can't trust him to not drop me.

"I don't know the name of the outpost," I tell him, "But it is the one that Zya, Fiske, Jasper, and Sylas live at. It is small and in Nightfang. Zuri lived there too before she kidnapped me and handed me over to the witch hunters."

Bade's wolf growls.

"Do you know where that is?"

It takes a moment but Bade chuffs. I am assuming that is an affirmative.

We run hard until nightfall when Bade finds a place to make camp for the night. He pulls some clothing out of a small bag that he had brought with him and gets dressed before making a fire and preparing the meat that he caught on our way here. Seeing him skin the animal probably would have turned my stomach if I hadn't been used to helping Juni do the same. It mostly just makes me miss her more.

Refusing to let him see me cry again, I quickly wipe my tears away and busy myself with filling my water pouch in the nearby stream.

We did not bring any bedding, so I prop myself up against a tree and stare at the flames, shivering in the cold.

After getting maybe an hour of poor sleep, Bade wakes me up so that we can continue our journey. We have not said a single thing to each other since I agreed to our travel arrangements the previous morning.

By the time the sun sets the second night, we are making our way into an outpost. We receive many curious looks, but nobody stops us as Bade carries me into a yurt style structure that I am assuming is our home for the night.

Once inside, I carefully climb from his back, making sure that the hem of the shirt that I am wearing does not ride up too high. Not only am I not wearing anything underneath, I have an embarrassing chafing situation happening on my inner thighs.

But I will just have to deal. I refuse to make this journey last any longer than necessary.

Bade shifts and I turn away, not wanting to see how frustratingly perfect he looks in his birthday suit.

"Someone will be in with hot water and some dinner. I will be outside if you need anything." Before he leaves, he softly adds, "Reese, I really am sorry."

I nod in response. Not trusting my voice. He can apologize until he is blue in the face, but it does not change anything.

I have never been with anyone before. I saved myself, feeling deep in my gut that I would find my person. The one person who I would share my life with. My everything with. I have never even been kissed. And then I am transported to this magical world where my literal soulmate lives. My soulmate who has visited me in my dreams for as long as I can remember. My soulmate who I saved myself for. My *one* person—and he doesn't want me. And I know, I know with everything that I am that I will never find another. He isn't choosing someone else over me. That would have hurt too—though I might have been able to understand if he was already in love with someone else. But that isn't it. There is no one else. He just doesn't want *me.*

I will just have to be okay with never experiencing that kind of love.

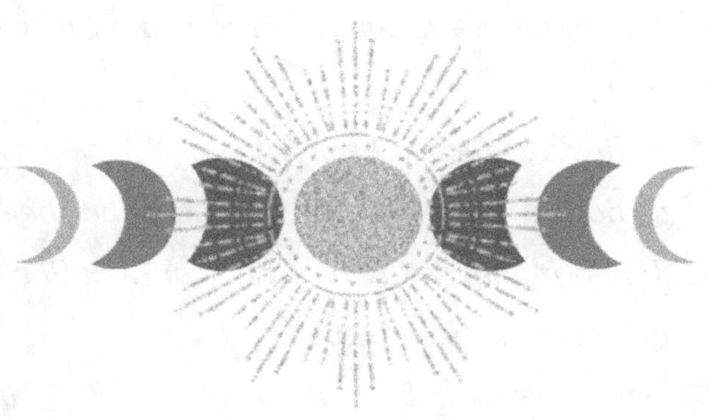

Chapter Ten

What the fuck am I doing? We have been traveling for four full days now and Reese has completely retreated within herself. The fire that she showed back in Tempest has extinguished. She cries silent tears and refuses to speak to me. I need some advice. I reach out to War, but swear him to secrecy before I share any of this with him. The last thing I need is Rowan knowing how spectacularly fucked up I have made things with her sister.

"I really need some. Reese has completely shut down. She will not talk to me. She does not even want me to be in the same room as her. I have been trying to

respect her space, but I listen to her cry, and I do not know what is wrong."

"Are her headaches back?"

"I do not think so. She usually holds her head when it hurts. When it gets really bad, she vomits. She has not been doing either of those things."

"Is she physically hurt in any other way? Have you checked her legs? Rowan's thighs were ripped open from rubbing on my fur during her first journey. Humans cannot heal quickly like we can."

"Fuck. I do not know. She is not going to let me look."

"Maybe send a female in with some salve to help her. Your saliva would work faster but if she isn't going to let you look, she certainly isn't going to let you lick."

"Why wouldn't she tell me if she was in pain?"

"Have you shown her that she is safe to be vulnerable with you?"

A gut-wrenching feeling tears at my stomach as my wolf continues to growl at me, telling me that this is all on me.

"No," I admit. "I have fucked up this entire situation."

"What did you do?"

"She found out that we are True Mates and I told her that I do not want a Mate."

"What the fuck, Bade? You rejected your Mate?"

"I did not reject her. I just told her that it cannot mean anything. You know I cannot have a Mate."

"Why the fuck not?"

"You saw what it did to our father. Losing our mother took everything from him. He could not be Alpha anymore. If I am not Alpha, our military is fucked. You keep everyone fed, Griff keeps everyone happy, and I keep everyone safe. It is how it works. I cannot fall apart when I lose her."

"If."

"What?"

"You said 'when I lose her.' It is an if. There are no guarantees. We all know that from experience. But rejecting your Mate is a pretty sure-fire way to ruin yourself and your Mate. How did your wolf even let you do that?"

"I did not reject her." I growl. "I have provided for her. I have kept her safe."

I can feel his scoff in my mind. "What did she say when you told her that you do not want a Mate?"

I sigh, fully understanding how fucked I have made this. "She told me that she has never been somebody's first

83

choice and all she has ever wanted is to be wanted.” My breathing becomes strained as I process the severity of my words. *“Fuck! How do I make this right?”*

“You need to pull your head out of your ass and realize that you have a True Mate. Then, you need to start acting like one. Be there for her. Get to know her. Stop rejecting her. Her heart is probably just as shredded as the skin on her thighs.”

I thank War for the advice, even though he only made me feel worse, and made him promise, again, that he will keep it to himself. Rowan is terrifying right now, and I do not want to be on her bad side—even this far away.

I was planning to have us camp in the forest tonight, but I adjust our route so that we can stop at an outpost with a healer. Wrath is the largest outpost within relative distance to our destination, so I head in that direction. Calling ahead to the healer that lives there, I request that she meets us at my lodging when we arrive. I also order food and hot water to be prepared and delivered ahead of our arrival. My head hurts from talking to War but I needed it. He is right. I cannot fight a True Mate bond. Our souls will pull us together regardless of whether I am ready or not.

All I am doing is hurting both of us.

When we get into my home at Wrath, I quickly shift and pull Reese into my arms so that she does not fall. I know that she must be in pain because she does not even try to protest being in my arms.

I gently set her down on the bed, careful of the wounds that I can smell have opened up. Now that I am allowing myself to pay attention. I am such a fucking fool. My Mate has been in physical pain for days and I was too caught up in my own shit to notice. My wolf would be tearing through my skin right now to properly care for her if he had a way to communicate with her without me.

I kneel in front of her and hold her hand in mine. Her hands are shaking, and she tries to turn away so that I cannot see the pain so clearly written on her face, but I am not going to allow that anymore.

No more hiding.

For either of us.

She can yell, scream, and fight but no more hiding.

"I am so sorry, Wildflower. I should have noticed that you were in pain. A healer will be here soon with some medicine for your legs. I will give you privacy while she examines you—but we are not doing this separately anymore. We are going to figure this out together. If you will let me, I want to explain to you why I was scared—am scared—about having a Mate. It is not that I do not want

85

you–you are beautiful, fiery, and brave. It is not that I do not choose you. I would choose you every time in every lifetime. I owe you an explanation and you will get one but first I need to make sure that you are no longer in pain, okay? Will you let a healer look at your thighs?"

"Okay," she agrees quietly after several minutes of silence. Her voice is hoarse, and it is the first word that she has spoken to me in days. But she agreed. Progress.

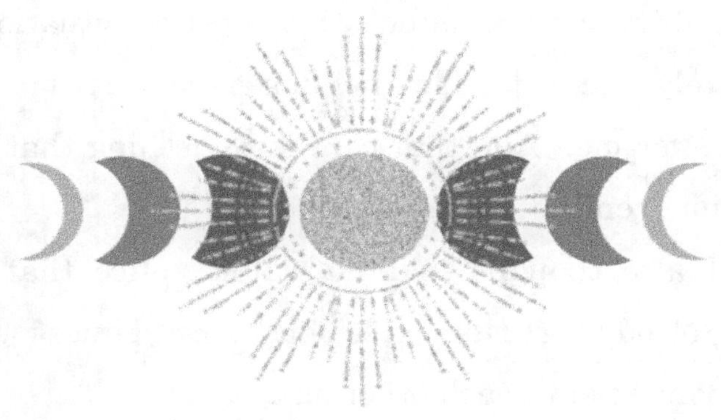

Chapter Eleven

I refuse to get my hopes up but after Bade's apology I decided that I don't have much of a choice but to admit that I am injured. I can't keep going like I have been. My thighs are in definite need of a healer. I am not sure what kind of medicine this healer is able to give me, but I am hoping that she is some kind of miracle worker. I quickly checked my legs after my bath last night and I am pretty sure that the wounds will leave scars.

I know that I should have said something to Bade about my legs. I was just so hurt by the entire situation that the pain in my legs was not a priority. Deep down, I knew that he would help me if I told him. But my feelings toward him and around this entire situation are completely jumbled. Bade helping me did not mean that he cares for me. And that care is something that I need from him even though I may never get it.

I also thought that he would notice that I was leaving bloody leg prints on his back. But I guess we were both trying to shut each other out.

The healer comes in and introduces herself as Tirza. Bade is about to leave when I call out to him. I do not understand why, but I know that I need him to stay. While I am pretty practiced at blocking out pain, having suffered from headaches my entire life—I am squeamish when it comes to blood and whatever else is probably leaking out of my wounds.

"Beast, can you stay?" The words come out quieter than I intend but he hears me anyway. Without hesitation, he walks back over and sits next to me on the bed. "I have gotten a little better about it since I arrived in this world, but I sometimes pass out when I see blood."

Bade lays a blanket over my lap so that I cannot see my wounds.

"Can you examine her like this?" he asks Tirza.

"Of course," she replies. Tirza's head disappears beneath the blanket, but she does not touch me at all. "These wounds should have healed themselves," she says.

"I am human," I tell her. "Humans do not heal as quickly as you do."

She looks up at Bade as if to question what I just told her. He nods.

"I heard about humans arriving in our world. I thought that it was just propaganda spread by those rebels."

"That's partly true," I tell her. "My sisters and I are not witches. The world that we came from does not have any magic at all."

"And you are all Mates to the Alphas?"

"Yes," Bade replies. Huh. I guess I knew that Ro was Mated to an Alpha, but I was unsure about Rams.

"I brought the strongest salve that I have. It should help numb the irritation while it heals. It would go faster if we added saliva to it."

"Spit?" Why would that help?

"Our saliva has healing properties. It cannot heal a large wound but is effective at helping skin heal faster. I did not suggest it earlier because I did not want you to feel uncomfortable. It would work best if I added it directly to the wound, but I can mix it into the salve if you would prefer," Bade explains.

"Directly? Meaning you would...oh. Oh! Um. Maybe we try it in the salve first," I reply shyly.

Tirza stifles a laugh as she reaches into her bag to pull out the salve. When her fingers brush mine, I feel a rush of tingles move from my chest up to my temples—right where the moon markings are. My vision goes dark, and I have no control over the words that come out of my mouth.

"Three full moons. Nightfang. An outpost two days northeast of the main village. Tall purple trees and a waterfall. Three moons. Nightfang. Two days northeast."

"Are you okay?" Bade turns my face so that he can look me over.

"What happened?" I try to shake off the lightheaded confusion that washed over me. Did I black out? It feels like I am just waking up.

"Your markings and eyes glowed and then you started giving directions to a place in Nightfang."

I shake my head again, trying to clear the slight fog that I am still in. After a few moments, things become clearer again.

"You need to follow those directions, Tirza. They will lead you to your True Mate." I do not know how, but I am certain that I am right. Tirza's Mate will be at the outpost that is two days northeast of the main village in Nightfang three full moons from now.

Tirza looks at me as if I just rattled off gibberish while my head spun around and I started foaming at the mouth. Apparently, this is the first time someone has had a magical vision in front of her. "He will be there," I tell her. "Your True Mate will be by the waterfall."

Bade is still holding my face, rubbing small circles at my temples. "Are you sure you are okay?"

"Yeah. I feel fine. It has never happened like that before. I have had visions, but they have only happened while I have been asleep. I have never been triggered by touching someone."

"Thank you, Alpha," Tirza says as she bows her head in respect for me. Weird, but okay. She leaves us with the salve and some clean fabric to bandage around my legs after the salve is applied.

When she is gone, Bade turns back to me. "Will you let me help you get into the bath and apply the salve after?"

The idea of him seeing my body makes me uncomfortable. And he can see that clearly on my face. But not for the reasons he is probably thinking. It is not that I feel unsafe around him or that I think he will do something inappropriate—it is just that no man has seen me naked before.

"I trust you. That is not what makes me nervous."

"I know that I have not earned it, but I do not want you to feel uncomfortable around me. What can I do?"

His words sound sincere, so I take a steadying breath and do my best to explain.

"I know that shifters are naked a lot—but that is not how it is back in New York. And I also know that you are probably way older than you look but I just turned 19 a few months ago. I'm sure that seeing my body is not a big deal to you when you have seen thousands before—but nobody has seen mine before."

Bade's eyes widened with surprise. "You are untouched?" he asks quietly.

I am immediately embarrassed that I just admitted that I am a big ol' virgin to my…whatever he is to me at this point. I have never even had this talk with my sisters.

I look away. Unable to look at him while admitting this. "Yes," I whisper.

He stares at me and takes deep breaths—but does not give any real indication as to how he feels about this information that I accidentally dropped at his feet.

"Can I ask why?" His question throws me off. I wasn't expecting it.

Because I am a hopeless romantic?

Because I wanted to save myself for the person who was meant to be my forever? You know, my soulmate. The guy who has already rejected me.

"It doesn't really matter anymore," I tell him. Because that is the truth. Whether he wants me or not, he is the only one that I could ever be with. I feel the truth of that in my bones.

I can tell that he does not like my non-answer, but he accepts it anyway.

"I promise that you are safe with me," he says. "I just want to help you."

Truthfully, I am not sure if I can even walk over to the bath at this point. I am going to need his help. So, I agree.

"Okay," I tell him softly.

He carefully picks me up and carries me over to the bathtub. Checking the temperature first, he must decide that it is okay because he lowers me into the water. I am still wearing his shirt, the fabric turning almost see-through as it clings to my skin. But I appreciate the gesture. He had added soap into the bath which stings my irritated skin, but I know that I need to keep it clean.

Bade methodically washes my hair, working through the many tangles in my curls. Once he is satisfied with that, he quickly braids my hair, securing it with a thin strip of leather, just like he secures his own Viking style braid down the center of his head.

After my bath, Bade lifts me from the tub and carries me over to the fire while he grabs a towel and a fresh shirt for me to wear.

"You can dry off and get dressed now," he tells me. "I will turn away to give you privacy."

I quickly pull the wet shirt over my head and use the towel to dry my body—biting my cheek when I accidentally rub my sore skin with the towel. I slip the dry shirt on and walk over to the bed.

I position myself so that my thighs are uncovered but the shirt still covers my center. I could probably apply the salve myself, but that would require looking at my legs and I can already feel my stomach churn at just the thought.

"I will be as gentle as I can, but this might sting just a little," he tells me as he kneels in front of me. I hear him suck in a sharp breath as he looks at me. "Fuck, Wildflower—you should have told me. No," he shakes his head, "I should have noticed. I am so sorry that you have been in so much pain."

It is a little thing, him taking some of the responsibility, but a small crack in my fractured heart is mended at his words.

He moves his hands lightly over my skin, applying the salve with as little pressure as possible.

"It isn't all your fault." I try to alleviate some of his guilt. "I didn't tell you. You had no way of knowing."

"If I would not have been so set on keeping my distance, I would have noticed. I should have assumed that this would happen. Rowan had a similar issue while traveling with my brother."

Knowing that Ro went through something similar makes me feel slightly less pathetic. "Did her legs get used to it or does it happen every time they travel?"

"He healed her with his saliva and then they had their bonding ceremony shortly after. Mate bonds allow magic to be shared so she now has quicker healing, like wolves do."

"Oh." Well, that isn't an option for me. He doesn't want a Mate—I doubt he would want to seal the bond with me just so that I heal faster. I wouldn't want that anyway. If I am going to tie myself to someone in that way, it will be because they *actually* want me. Not just because there isn't another option. "I guess I will just have to hope that my skin toughens up a bit, then."

After the ointment is applied, Bade wraps my legs in the bandages and then grabs the tray of food that was brought to us. My stomach rumbles, making me realize that I haven't really eaten all day.

"Please eat," he asks quietly. "I will have more food brought in. I just realized that I didn't even stop at all to let you eat today." He curses quietly to himself. "I will do better."

"Please don't beat yourself up about this. I am okay. And I am no stranger to hunger. I have been in worse pain, and I have gone longer without food." I was trying to make the situation better, but he did not like what I just said. His eyes darken and a loud growl rumbles from his chest.

"You will never go hungry again," he declares firmly. "Your legs should start to heal soon, but we will stay at this outpost until your wounds are gone. Try to get some sleep." He pulls away from me and stalks towards the door.

"Wait," I tell him. "Where are you going?"

"I need to meet with a few pack members while I am here. I will be right outside."

"Okay." I nod my head. "Thank you...for helping me."

"You do not ever need to thank me, sweetheart. I should have been helping you all along."

With that, he turns and leaves. Only this time, I do not feel so alone.

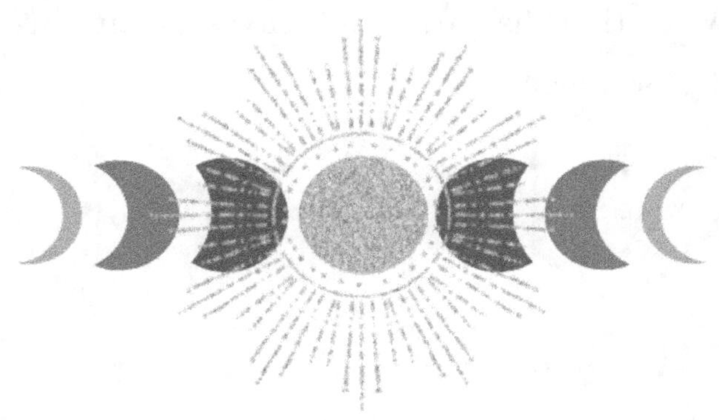

Chapter Twelve

We stayed at Wrath for three days while my legs healed. Honestly, they are still not completely there—but I need to get to Juni. The days are warming, and I promised her that I would return when the weather was nice.

Bade gave me a pair of leather pants to wear—hopefully they will help my legs while we do this next stretch of travel. We will be making camp tonight and then we should make it to the outpost late tomorrow night. Bade made me promise that I would tell him when I needed to stop for a break to eat or go to the bathroom. He is still mad at himself for not thinking of those needs earlier.

While we were at Wrath, Bade was able to get an update on Dreena and Briggs. According to Boone, they are no longer together. Dreena was spotted moving from the Bear territory into the Panther territory with a large group of her followers who fled. Briggs was not with them.

I wake in the night sweating and panting from the dirtiest dream I have ever had. It is something that has been happening more and more since I started spending time with Bade. My situationship that I have with him is straight out of the many romance books that I would read back in New York. All of my favorite tropes are playing out in front of me in real time. It is no wonder my brain is creating spicy scenes for us as well. We have Grumpy/Sunshine, forced proximity, fated mates. Would me riding on his wolf's back count as one-horse? I snort at the thought. How is this my life?

Bade is lying next to me in his wolf form. I cannot tell if he is asleep or not, but now that I am awake, I really need to pee.

Not wanting to wake him if he is asleep, I slowly rise from my spot and creep around to the other side of a tree. I see his ears flick in my direction, so he must be awake. That is something that I have had to get used to—

Bade listening while I relieve myself. The first few times that I tried to pee in the woods, I got stage fright. I couldn't do it. It was different when I was with Juni—or even when I was held prisoner. With Bade, there is a level of intimacy in everything that we do—even if we ignore it. So, I pretend that I am in a bathroom stall at Target. Others can hear me pee then too and it doesn't bother me. Why should this be any different? That is the speech I have to give myself every time, but at least it works.

The next time I wake up, it is nearly morning, and I am embarrassingly using Bade as a body pillow. Somehow in the night, I turned my body around, closed the large gap that I left between our bodies, and am full on big-spooning him. He is still in his wolf form, thank god, but I scramble to pull myself away from him.

"Sorry," I mumble.

His wolf chuffs a laugh and then grabs a pair of pants and scampers off into the woods out of sight. We do this routine every morning—well, not the mortifying snuggling part—so I know that he is going to pee and then shift and dress to help me clean up our camp and inhale some breakfast before we head out again.

"For the record, Wildflower, you can use my body however you need any time that you want." He has a smug smile on his face. I squeeze my thighs together at the thought. My feelings for Bade are very confusing and complicated, but there is no denying my attraction for him. I have had crushes before, but this feels like so much more. Ever since his apology he has been more open about his feelings and attraction towards me as well. Over the last few days, he has begun to flirt with me—and the line that he had previously placed between us. *I would choose you in every lifetime.*

I scoff and try to hide my matching smile, but it breaks through anyway.

"I like you better as a wolf," I grumble.

He throws his head back and laughs and I realize that it is the first time that he has laughed like that around me. Warmth spreads through my chest, hope rising again that maybe we can figure this out after all.

Before we left, he let me know that he spoke with his brothers last night while I was sleeping. Dreena is dead. Ramsey killed her. I cannot imagine the heartache that my sister must be feeling. Being a nurse, she has always been the one to save a life, not take one. From what Bade was told, it happened in self-defense. I am so thankful that she was able to defend herself and that Dreena is finally done hurting people. But I know that Ramsey will have wanted to save her. She would have seen the fractures in Dreena's mind and would have wanted to get her the help that she needs.

Dreena is gone but the threat is still out there because Briggs is still missing.

Briggs, who was poisoning Dreena's mind.

Briggs, who had threatened to force a bond and himself on me so that he could steal my magic.

Honestly, I couldn't think about any of that right now.

"Will we still make it to the outpost tonight?" I look up at the sky and see storm clouds.

"Yes. We will have to run through the storm, but we might as well push through. It is the closest outpost to us."

And storm it did. I press my body as close to Bade's back as I can while he tears through the forest. The trees offer little protection from the downpour and wind. Branches are flung wildly in the wind—one whipping me across the cheek. I let out a pained gasp, catching Bade's attention, but urge him to keep going.

About twenty minutes before we arrive at the outpost, the storm dies down. I am so cold and sore from shivering and holding onto Bade, that I cannot even move properly to climb down from his back once we do arrive. Muscles that I didn't even know I have scream at me in protest. Bade shifts and catches me. Cursing as he holds me close to his body, offering his body heat as I shake in his arms.

We are greeted by Fiske as we enter the camp. He must have been on watch for the night. He asks me if I want him to wake Juni but given the mess that I currently am, I tell him that we will see her in the morning. I need to get my body functional again first.

Bade takes us to one of the larger yurt structures. It is similar to the one that Juni and I stayed in when I was here last, but it is bigger. If I had to guess, I would say that this is his brother's home here.

Bade gets right to work, building a fire in the large center ring in the yurt. He begins heating water for a bath. He must be exhausted as well but he is going to make sure that I am taken care of before he rests. And I will let him. Somewhere along this journey, things have begun to shift between us. I do not know what any of it means. I do not know if he has changed his mind about wanting me to be his Mate. But I am too tired to ask right now.

I strip out of my soaked clothes without even thinking. His pupils are blown out as I walk past him, but he doesn't say anything. He just finishes filling the bathtub, adding some soaps and oils for me to use.

I can't help the moan that comes out of my mouth as I sink into the hot water. I hear a sharp intake of breath but then he leaves the yurt. Bade returns with some food as I am getting myself out of the bath. While I sit by the fire and start to eat, Bade strips out of his clothes and heads for the tub, dumping one more hot bucket of water in before climbing in himself.

I feel myself biting my lip as I watch him. It is the first time that I have allowed myself to look—other than that quick glance after I tripped over him in the hall. God, his body is perfect. He has more muscles than I thought humanly possible.

Every inch of him is hard and huge.

Every.

Goddamn.

Inch.

His skin is bronzed from hours spent out in the sun. He takes the braid out of his hair, washing his long blond strands before tying it up in a man-bun on the top of his head. His hair is shaved on the sides of his skull, making his moon marking even more striking on his skin. He has abstract swirls of tattoos all over his chest, arms, and back. The silvery moon tattoo shimmers on his temple as it catches light from the fire. It is beautiful. *He* is beautiful.

"Do you like what you see, Wildflower?" His question startles me out of my blatant ogling. Do I have drool on my face? I feel my face heat at being called out, but I cannot look away.

"Yes," I admit. He chuckles. "I was actually just thinking about how strange it is to see you in person. For so long, you only lived in my dreams."

"How does that work, anyway?"

"No clue. I don't seem to have any control over it. You saw what happened with the healer. I didn't do anything to make that happen."

"We can try to figure it out once we get back to the lodge. Rowan is already there, and it sounds like Ramsey will be back around the same time that we get there— depending on how long it takes to travel with Juni."

"She won't slow us down at all," I assure him. "She is only four, but her grandmother taught her a lot before she passed. She had been living on her own for a while before she found me. Honestly, she is the reason I was able to survive for my first months here."

"You said that her heart string brought her to you?"

"Yeah. That is how she described it. I obviously do not know much about bear shifters, but it sounds like it is the same as what the True Mate soul pull feels like. Sylas guessed that it was the same thing, anyway. Since magic is often felt in the chest, the bears just associate it with the heart instead of the soul. Sylas's wolf felt the same pull towards her."

Bade gets out of the tub, slinging a towel around his waist before joining me by the fire. I watch as beads of water glide down his body, distracted once more.

Shaking myself free from my not so platonic thoughts, I refocus on our conversation. "Juni told me that her grandmother had visions too. Before she died, she told Juni to follow her heart string. It led her into Nightfury where she found me and then into Nightfang where we found Sylas."

"Visions like you have?" he questions.

"I think so. She had hers during the day though. Juni called her a daydreamer." I laugh. "I'm not sure if that is an official title or just a four-year-old trying to make sense of the world."

"My grandmother might know more about bear shifters than we do. She is nearing 1000 and has traveled a lot in her lifetime."

1000? "Will she be at the lodge too?"

"Yes. She is our primary healer—though Ramsey might be taking over that role now that she is bonded and has access to her magic."

"She would be a healer even without magic."

"I'm sure she would. But from what I hear, her magic is pretty incredible. She was able to heal Rowan after she was attacked. Saved her life and the life of her babies."

I gasp. "Ro was attacked and is pregnant?"

"Fuck," Bade presses his palms to his eyes. "I probably should have shared that with you sooner. Yes, she was attacked but my father killed the attacker. Ramsey healed her and she is okay now. And, yes, she is pregnant. Triplets."

"Does Ro have magic too—other than faster healing?"

"Yes. Both of your sisters are Moon Touched like you."

"I thought you said it is rare?"

"It is. It was just the stuff in legends before the three of you showed up. Rowan likes to believe that she has a magic pussy." He chuckles as he says it.

I snort. "Of course she does. She probably thought that before the moon magic, though."

"In reality, she is able to increase fertility. It is something that our wolves have been struggling with for a while. I think that the three of you were brought here to help us fix it. Rowan can help increase pregnancy rates, Ramsey can help mothers and babies survive the birth, and you...well, if the vision that you had with the healer is any indication, I think that you can help wolves find their Mates."

Could that be true? I can't help but believe that I was destined to be here since I have been dreaming of Bade for my entire life. I clean up our dishes and crawl into bed while Bade adds another log to the fire.

"Will you lay with me tonight?" I ask timidly. "As your wolf, I mean. I am still feeling cold."

"Of course, sweetheart. I will be over in a minute."

That is when I realize that I do not have any clothes to wear. I am still wrapped in the towel from my bath. Fuck it. He has seen it all now anyway and I am too tired to do anything about it.

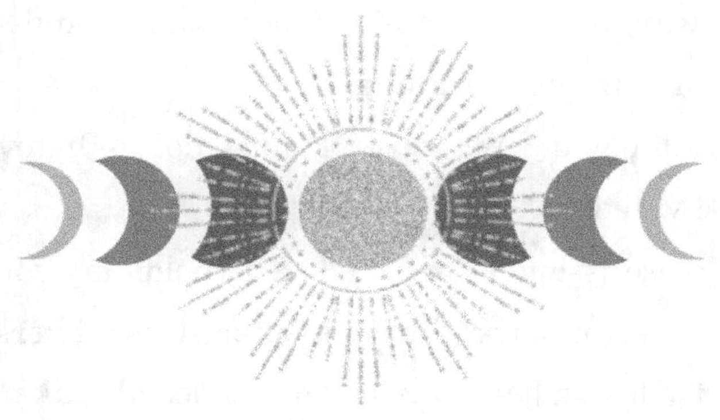

Chapter Thirteen

There is no way that I am getting any sleep tonight. Reese has her perfect, naked body wrapped around me, and I cannot think of anything else. It started out innocently enough—she fell asleep wrapped in nothing but her towel—but kept to her side of the bed. Until she didn't. Now, her soft, creamy skin is pressed up against my body. Her towel? Lost somewhere within the blankets.

All my effort is being placed into making sure that I do not shift out of my wolf form. I will give her the warmth and comfort that she requested—even if it kills me.

She is untouched. A virgin. No other man has felt her. Seen her. Had her. And she is mine. I just need to find a way to fix all the damage that I did to our relationship in the beginning.

But I will. Whatever I must do. Whatever she needs. I will do it.

Reese is my True Mate. She holds my soul. My heart. Everything that I have to offer. It is all hers. I am terrified of losing her. Terrified of the heartbreak that lies ahead if I were to lose her. So, I will just need to do everything that I can to keep her safe.

She is becoming more comfortable around me. Even in her sleep, her body knows that she is safe with me. That is why she is clinging to me now. She looks so peaceful while she dreams. Her mouth parted slightly. A soft snore escapes every now and then, making me smirk.

She has a mark across her cheek that must have been caused by a branch in the storm. I know that she sleeps soundly so I quickly lick over the scratch. She should be healed by the time she wakes up in the morning.

I cannot sleep but I allow myself to dream anyway. In my dream, I take Reese to the water's edge by the lodge. I bond with her under the full moon, and we become a family.

The two of us *and* Juni.

I have yet to meet this little girl but when Reese talks about her, I feel in my soul that she is mine too.

Our family lodge, which has been haunted by ghosts for so long, is once again filled with life. War and Rowan's pups will play in the garden with Juni while Reese's belly swells with pups of our own. Our family thrives. Our packs thrive.

I dream of happiness. Peace. Love. Things that I never thought I would experience. I can try to fight it–I *did* try to fight it–but Reese is in my marrow. My heart. My soul. I would do anything for her. Which is why I will be honest with her about my fears and hope that she is able to forgive me for how idiotic I was when we first met.

But for now, I will hold her while she sleeps, and I will let myself dream.

Reese stretches awake as the sun is just starting to rise. I climb out of bed and shift on my way to the fire, grabbing Reese's now dry shirt for her to put on. She bites her lip, and she stares at my bare ass. I cannot help the smirk that appears on my own face.

"Good morning, Wildflower. Did you sleep okay?"

"Yes, thank you," she replies as she pulls the shirt over her head. "Hey, Bade? I realized last night that I never even asked you about your feelings with Juni. I know that you do not even want a Mate so I'm guessing kids weren't really on your radar and now you are kind of getting both. I mean...if that is what you even want." Her voice gets quieter as she says those last words. She asks about Juni, but she is really questioning if I want *her*.

I cross back over to her, sitting next to her on the bed. She tries to look away, nervous about what I might say, but we are not hiding anymore so I turn her face towards me.

"Sweetheart, I know that this did not start as it should have. And that is completely my fault. I will always regret the pain that I caused your heart, and I will do anything, everything that I can to make up for it. But I…I have always been afraid of having a Mate. Afraid of what it would do to me if I lost you. I know that I tried to fight it in the beginning, but you *are* my Mate, Reese. And I will spend the rest of my days showing you that I can do better. I can be who you need me to be."

"Why were you afraid?"

"My parents were True Mates. My mother died during childbirth when my brothers and I were young. The pups that she was carrying passed too. Losing my mother broke my father. He was Alpha to all three packs, and he could not do it anymore. If my uncle, his Beta, had not stepped in to carry the load, it could have meant the end to the pack. Still to this day, my father is a shell of the man he once was. Though, he is starting to come back bit by bit. I think that having life at the lodge again will be good for him. But that is why I was afraid."

"I'm sorry that you went through that. Sometimes I think that I had it easier than my sisters because I don't remember our parents at all."

I reach out and hold her hand. "You never should have had to go through that. Rowan has shared a bit about what your life was like, and I am happy that you had your sisters."

"Me too. And that is part of the reason why Juni is so important to me. The fact that I have dreamt of her my entire life aside, she needs a family, and I know that I am a part of that—we are a part of that—but you need to be okay with it too. I will not force you to have a relationship with anybody. I..."

"I am excited to meet her today," I say, cutting her off. "I'm a little nervous, if I am honest. I thought about everything a lot last night. I do not know much about kids—next to nothing about bear shifter kids—but I know that you are a package deal. She is important to you and therefore she is important to me. I would never make you feel like you have to choose or keep parts of your life separate."

Before I even know what is happening, Reese wraps her hand around the back of my neck and seals her lips to mine. The kiss is hesitant and over way too quickly. She pulls away as a beautiful flush colors her cheeks. Needing more, I cup her face in my hands and kiss her again. She sighs against my mouth and when I trace my tongue over the crease in her lips, begging for entry, she parts them for me. Her lips are so soft, and they taste so fucking sweet. I keep it slow, but deepen the kiss, moving my tongue over hers until she is moaning for more. Her taste, her sounds, the feel of her lips pressed to mine—it all settles my soul. Like after years of surviving, I am finally starting to live.

Hearing that we are about to have a visitor, I end the kiss and quickly pull some pants on. I turn away from the door and finish fastening them up right as a little girl with brown hair and golden eyes runs through our door. I do not think she even notices that I am here as she charges straight toward Reese and flings herself into my Mate's waiting arms.

"You came back!" she says against Reese's neck. Her voice is as tiny as she is. Her golden eyes twinkle with unshed tears as she hugs Reese tightly.

"I promised I would, honey," Reese replies. They are both crying happy tears.

"My apologies, Alpha," Sylas says, pulling my attention away from the happy reunion. "I told her to ask before she came in."

"It is okay," I tell him as I hold my arm out in greeting. "She is always welcome."

"Who are you?" Juni asks as she tilts her head to the side.

Reese snorts. "Juni, this is Bade. He is my Mate. He brought me back to you. Bade, this is Juniper," she introduces with a beaming smile.

I walk over to them and crouch down, so I am at eye level. I extend my hand out like I just did with Sylas. "It is nice to finally meet you, Princess. Reese has told me so much about you."

"Did she tell you I'm a bear?"

I chuckle. "Yes."

"Did she tell you I'm a good hunter?"

"She told me that you saved her when she needed help. That was very brave of you."

"Sylas told me we're going to live at the lodge in the main village with Reese's sisters. Is that where you live too?"

"Yes. The lodge is my family's home."

"You an Alpha?"

I chuckle again. "Yes. I am the Alpha of Nightfury."

"Are there kids to play with at the lodge? 'Cause I made a friend named Jasper and I like to play a lot."

"There are no other kids that live at the lodge yet, but there are hundreds of kids in the main village. And Reese's sister is going to have her babies soon. They will live at the lodge once they are born."

She taps her chin like she is thinking really hard about something. "Okay!"

Reese snuggles Juni tighter, and they curl up in bed as Juni tells her about everything that she has done while she was away. I nod for Sylas to follow me outside.

"Thank you for caring for her while Reese was gone. I know that was not an easy decision for her to make and the entire thing was sprung on you suddenly."

"I will always be there to protect Juni."

"You are welcome to come with us to the main village. I am sure that your wolf will demand it. We will find accommodations near the lodge for you to stay in. We have several lodgings on our grounds. They were once used for staff, but we do not have staff living on site anymore. We can get you set up with everything that you need."

"I would appreciate that. Zya made some clothing for Juni. I will pack our items in a bag for our move. I would like to learn more about bear shifters, if there are any books about them. Juni has not told me much about their customs. I thought that they lived in clans, but it sounds like she lived alone with her grandmother. All I really know right now is that she prefers to stay in this form most of the time but almost always sleeps as a bear."

"Her grandmother might have taught her to sleep in bear form for safety. We will figure it out together. My brother keeps an extensive library at the lodge. And Heka and my father might know some things too. We will ask them."

Just then, a young wolf pup comes tearing across the camp, shifts, and starts pounding on my legs as tears fill his eyes. "Please don't take her. She is my friend!"

I get down on his level as his mother comes running towards us. Hearing the commotion, Reese brings Juni outside as well.

"I am so sorry, Alpha," Zya says, trying to pull her squirming son away from me.

"It is okay," I wave her off.

"I gots ta leave with my family, Jas," Juni tells him, pulling him into a hug. Reese kneels down next to me.

"We would love for you to come and visit," she tells him. "And we can plan a time for us to come back here too. Juni will still be your friend even if she lives in another village."

Reese reaches out and holds both of their hands. Her moon markings and eyes start to glow. Everyone gasps.

"Do not worry," I say quietly, calmly. "She is having a vision."

Reese begins to mutter words as the light in her eyes pulses. "A child. Not a wolf. A cub—a panther cub. Cold. A party at the lodge? Two years."

The glow fades and she sucks in a deep breath.

"What did that mean?" Sylas asks.

"I believe that is when Jasper will find his True Mate," she tells him, slightly out of breath. I rub gentle circles on her back as she leans into me.

"If it is a party at the lodge while the weather is cold, it must be our family's winter solstice celebration," I explain. Turning to Jasper and his family I add with a smile, "It looks like you all are invited for a solstice party in two years."

With a plan to head out in the morning, we spend the rest of the day at the outpost, allowing Juni and Jasper time to play while Reese and I help hunt, prepare meals, and pack for the final leg of our journey.

I would like to continue our discussion from the morning, but as I enter War's lodging after dinner, I find Reese asleep in bed with a small bear cub curled up in her arms. I add another log to the fire and crawl into bed behind Reese, laying a protective arm across both of my girls. At this moment, I know with absolute certainty that they are my world, and I will do anything to keep them safe.

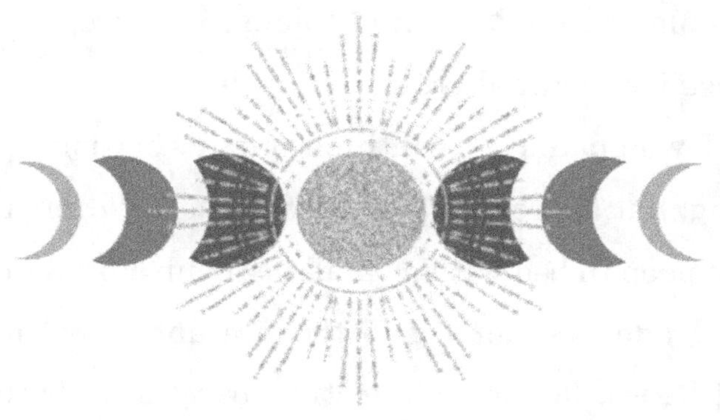

Chapter Fourteen

(Present Day)

"And now we are here," I say, looking at my family. I cannot believe that my sisters are both here, Mated to wolf shifters, and Ro is about to pop out triplets. Our lives look drastically different from the ones that we left back in New York.

"The visions must be part of the Moon Touched magic," Ramsey says. "And you can have them even though you are not Mated? Is that possible?" She looks over at Griffin.

"You healed Rowan before we were Mated," he tells her.

"Yeah, but then my magic was completely gone. I could not feel it anymore until after our ceremony."

"I don't feel magic at all," I tell them. "At least not until a vision has already taken over my body. I have no idea how it happens. I have no control over it."

"There must be something that triggers the magic," Griffin says as he takes a book from his father's hands. Finding the page that he was looking for, he re-reads the passage that they were discussing when I first entered the kitchen. "And there were Three Goddesses of The Moon. Born among man. Awakened by love. To bear, mend, and find. To restore the balance. To replenish The Mother. Divided; together once more. Hearts will bind."

"Love," Bade's father says. "Forceful, all-encompassing love is what triggered their magic."

"Yes, but I think that it is more than that," Bade says.

Griffin makes a noise of agreement. "It was the first time that the *needed* to use their magic. Or, at least, when their magic felt like it was needed."

"So, my magic was triggered during the fuck fest because I love War *and* there were wolves nearby who wanted to become pregnant?" Ro says.

Ramsey nods. "And mine was triggered because I love Ro and *needed* to heal her."

"And mine was triggered because I *needed* to see how to save Juni." I sneak a quick glance at Bade, not wanting to admit out loud that the vision also told me where I would find him—or rather, where he would find me. Maybe the love that I felt wasn't completely for Juni. "That vision was different from the others that I have had since, though. I was able to see several different scenarios, all with different outcomes. It isn't like that anymore."

"Maybe because you aren't bonded yet?" Ro suggests. "My magic was different before I bonded. And Ramsey had magic to save me but then it was gone until she bonded."

"Maybe," I shrug. Looking over at my little girl as she drools peacefully on the sofa. That first vision just felt different.

"And your migraines, are they better?" Ramsey asks.

"Yes. I still have headaches, but I haven't had a migraine in a little while."

"Can I have a look?" she asks me. "I am going to check on Ro's babies first but as long as I don't feel a strain in my power, I can check you over too."

"I would like that," I tell her. I am not sure what she will be able to find, but it is worth a shot. Maybe there is even a medication here that could help manage my symptoms.

"What will you be able to see? Is it going to gross you out to see my guts?" Ro asks Rams.

"Absolutely not," she laughs. "I want to make sure that the babies are positioned correctly and check to see if there are any tears or weak spots that might cause issues later. I can also see if you are having boys or girls, how much hair they have, how big they are…"

"You can give me an ultrasound with your mind? War!" Ro squeals as she smacks his shoulder. "We get to have an ultrasound!"

"I heard, love." He chuckles as he places a kiss on the top of her head. "You will really be able to tell us the sex?"

"Yep. I practiced a bit while we were visiting outposts in Nighthowl. It should only take a few minutes."

"Well, let's do it!" Ro says as she claps her hands together excitedly.

I watch in awe as Ramsey places her hand over Rowan's rounded belly. Her hands and eyes glow with a silvery light.

"Is that what I look like when I am having a vision," I ask Bade quietly.

"Yes, Wildflower. But the light comes from your eyes and temples."

"Freaky."

He snorts and playfully squeezes my side.

After a couple of minutes, the magical glow dims and Ramsey pulls her hand away.

"Everything looks perfect, Ro. I think you probably have about another month left before they are cooked enough to come out, though shifter due dates are not my expertise."

Everyone in the room lets out a breath of relief.

"Are you ready to find out the genders?"

We all nodded, eager to learn everything that we can.

"You are having two boys and one girl. The little girl already has a thick head of dark hair like her daddy. One of the boys was in his wolf form. His fur was blond. The other boy was completely bald—so we will have to wait and see what his coloring will be." We all chuckle despite the tears in our eyes.

"And they are healthy?" Bade's father asks.

"Completely healthy. All four of them."

We all jump up and exchange hugs.

"I can't believe that you are going to be a mom," I tell Ro as I hug her.

"I can't believe you are already a mom," she says in return. "And don't think that I didn't notice the sexual tension between you and the hunky warrior. We will be discussing that later."

"I don't know what you are talking about," I whisper-shout back.

She snorts. "Sure you don't."

Needing to change the subject, I turn to Ramsey. "What do you say? Want to have a look and see what I have floating around up here," I point to my head.

"Hopefully nothing is floating. I will need to look at your trigeminal nerve—though based on the location of your moon markings, I'm guessing I already know the cause," she explains.

I nod my understanding as she walks closer. Bade pulls me down to sit next to him while I close my eyes. Ramsey's touch is gentle as she places her hands over my temples. She lingers for only a minute before pulling away again.

"Bade," she turns her attention to him, "Griffin told me that you suffer from headaches as well. Would you mind if I have a look?"

"Of course," he tells her, confusion coloring his words.

"I have a hunch," she tells him as she reaches for his temples next.

When she pulls away again, she is nodding to herself.

"Griffin told me that you have a heightened sense of sight. You can see further than other wolves and also have thermal vision, correct?"

"Yes," he confirms.

"For both of you, I believe that your headaches are related to the Moon Touched magic that was gifted. The nerve cluster that is most likely causing you pain, is lit up silver."

"So, we will just have to deal with the headaches?" I ask. I try to hide the disappointment in my voice, though it comes through anyway. "That is okay. We can do that."

"I think the headaches might go away once you bond," Ramsey says.

"I think so too," Griffin adds, coming up to Ramsey's side. "For Rowan and Ramsey, their powers were unreliable until after our bonding. Rowan's magic altered the weather without anyone knowing that it was happening, Ramsey was able to use her magic to save Rowan but then her well of magic was unable to replenish itself. You are receiving visions but do not have any control over them when they happen. Did the headaches happen after a vision?"

"Maybe." Did they? "Up until very recently, I thought the visions were just dreams. I have only had two while awake."

"Like Nana," a small voice says. Juni sits up and rubs her eyes before crawling up into my lap. "Nana was a daydreamer too. But her eyes shined gold. Like sunshine."

"Like your eyes," Bade tells her as he boops her on her nose, making her giggle.

"Juni, do you have dreams too?" I ask her.

"Just of you. All of you. Sylas too. And Jasper. He is my best friend forever."

Ramsey crouches down to be at eye level with Juni. "Would it be okay if I checked you over too? Just like I did with Reese and Bade? You won't feel anything other than my hands on the sides of your head."

Juni looks to me and then to Bade. We both give her encouraging nods. "Okay," she says with a shrug.

Ramsey gently holds Juni's tiny face in her hands and pushes a small amount of magic into her. She nods and then pulls her hands away.

"Just like you, but gold. I do not know what the bear-shifter equivalent is to being Moon Touched, but I think that is what is going on. She has similar gifts."

"Sun Kissed," Griffin says.

"What?" I ask.

"Sun Kissed. That is the bear shifter equivalent to being Moon Touched. I read about it a long time ago in a book on legends."

Tears fill my eyes, overwhelmed by all of this information. Bade pulls me, with Juni, onto his lap and tucks my face into his neck.

"I'm okay, Reese, I promise," Juni tells me. "It dinnit give me an owie."

"That's not why I'm crying, honey bear. I am just so happy that we found each other so that we can figure this all out together."

"Why did you let me eat all of the cobbler?" Rowan asks War as she wipes the tears from both their eyes, "This is totally a cobbler moment."

"You think every moment is a cobbler moment," he replies. When she hits him playfully, he adds, "but of course you are right, love."

"Nice save," Bade snorts as he wipes the tears from my cheeks.

Bade's father mumbles something as he leaves the room and then returns with a full pan of cobbler.

Ro gasps. "Lycus! Where did you find that?!"

"If I did not hide it, I would never get to eat any. It is *my* favorite dessert, you know," he tells her.

"I will let it slide this once because I love you and you helped save my life but don't think for one second that I won't have Griff and Rams sniff out your hiding spots next time I run out."

"I would expect nothing else," he tells her with a laugh.

Later that afternoon, Bade leaves the lodge to get Sylas set up in one of the cabins located on the property. He will be living there and will be added to a local hunting party so that he can stay close while Juni grows. Because of her age, his wolf will be content with this arrangement.

After dinner in the garden, Bade brings Juni and I to his wing of the lodge. In addition to his master suite, there is an office and an extra bedroom with an attached bathroom. I give Juni a bath while Bade sets her bed up with additional blankets and pillows. Griffin and Ramsey bring a pile of children's stories from the library, and Rowan and War drop off a teddy bear that they had purchased at the market for her on their afternoon stroll.

We get her tucked in, making sure that she knows we will be right down the hall, and then I snuggle up with her while Bade reads us a story.

After she falls asleep, Bade and I kiss her on her forehead and then quietly leave her room. Watching how gentle he is with her makes my heart flutter. He had told me that he wants this–us–our family. But saying and seeing are two completely different things.

We haven't spoken about our relationship since Juni burst through our door at the outpost. I keep replaying our kiss in my head–the first kiss that I have ever had–and all I know is that I want more.

I have no idea what I am doing. I know that Bade and I need to talk, but I need to talk to my sisters first.

Bade and I return to the central living room after putting Juni to bed. Ramsey, Griffin, Rowan, and War all look up as we walk in the room.

"What's going on?" I ask hesitantly.

"Well, normally, we would be having family game night," Rowan explains. "But we thought that we might skip it tonight so that Rams and I can steal you away and get the tea."

"What tea?" Bade asks, confused.

"She means information. She wants to grill me about you," I explain with a slight smirk.

"We can make sure that there is tea, if you think you need it," Ramsey says with a wink.

"What does that mean?" I ask, confused.

"If you are at all not ready to add to your little family, I highly suggest you and Bade both drink the tea. My magic pussy broadcasts good vibes without me even trying, if you know what I mean," Ro explains.

My face instantly heats. I hadn't even thought about birth control. Ramsey offered to help me get a prescription for birth control back in New York, but I had no need for it. I am not sure what is happening with Bade and me, but I have a feeling that things will progress in that direction. I want it to. I think. I'm pretty sure. Does he want it to? He does...right?

"Breathe, Wildflower," Bade leans down to whisper in my ear. "We can talk about all of that later."

I gulp and nod. I am so inexperienced.

"I would say don't wait up," Ramsey says to the guys as she grabs my hand and starts pulling me from the room, "but we all know you will anyway."

War pulls Ro into an almost indecent kiss before she scurries out of the room with us.

My sisters bring me to a secret room that they call "The Hideaway" so that we can have a bit of privacy.

"Spill," Ro says as we sit down on the plush furniture.

Ramsey snorts.

"I have no idea what I am doing. I have never…"

"That's okay," Ramsey tells me gently.

"When he first found me, I was so sick. Then, when I was feeling better, he was avoiding me because he did not want a Mate. Now, he seems to want it all and he is so good with Juni and we kissed one time but nothing else has happened and he knows that I have never… but he didn't really say anything when I told him and I just really don't know what I'm doing or what to expect or how in the world his giant dick is ever going to fit in any part of me…if that is something that he even wants with me. I think he does but we haven't talked about it."

"Okay," Ro says. "We are going to unpack that bit by bit. Who initiated the kiss?"

"I did. But I didn't know what I was doing so I pulled away." My face must be as red as a tomato. It isn't even that I am embarrassed to talk to my sisters about this. We have always told each other everything. But what if I am making a bigger deal out of our kiss than it was? Bade has surely been kissed hundreds of times before. How am I going to measure up?

"What did he do after you pulled away?" Ramsey asks.

"He kissed me again. But it was more. Deeper. It was perfect. But then Juni came rushing in and he pulled his pants on, and we haven't talked about it at all."

"He didn't have pants on?" Ro asks with a smirk.

"Well, he had just shifted before we started talking..."

"Okay. And when you were kissing, what was happening with his trouser snake?" she asks.

"He was hard. I think. I tried not to look but I don't think he is ever not hard. Is that normal? Oh my god. I don't even know if it is normal?" I cover my face with my hands, trying to hide my embarrassment. "I assume men can't be hard all of the time, right? Why didn't I pay more attention in Sex Ed?"

"Because Mr. Lloyd was about as interesting as a root canal." Ro says.

"Typically, men cannot stay hard all the time," Ramsey says gently. "But our men are anything but typical. I think it is more of a True Mates thing than a shifter thing, though."

"Okay. But I really don't think that it, he, will fit anywhere. Have you seen our size difference? He is huge. And, if he is somehow able to fit without splitting me in half, won't he crush me with his muscles? His muscles have muscles!"

"Breathe, kiddo," Ramsey tells me. "When you are ready, he will fit. But you just need to talk to him. If he already knows that you are inexperienced, I'm sure that he is waiting for you to show him that you are ready for the next steps. And, if you just stay at the kissing stage for a while, that is okay too. We were made for our Mates, and they were made for us."

"Are you ready for the next step?" Ro asks gently.

"I don't know what I am ready for. All I know is that when I think about our kiss, I want more. More kisses. Maybe more other things too."

"Just take it slow," Ramsey replies.

"Do what feels right in the moment," Ro adds.

My sisters and I catch up until Ro falls asleep mid-sentence. Ramsey contacts Griffin and a few minutes later, all three guys quietly walk into the hideaway. War gently scoops Rowan up into his arms as Griffin and Ramsey lead us out.

Feeling braver after talking to my sisters, I reach out and hold Bade's hand. He lifts our intertwined fingers to his mouth and places a light kiss on my knuckles before walking me to our wing of the lodge.

I can't help the huge grin that graces my face. He wants this.

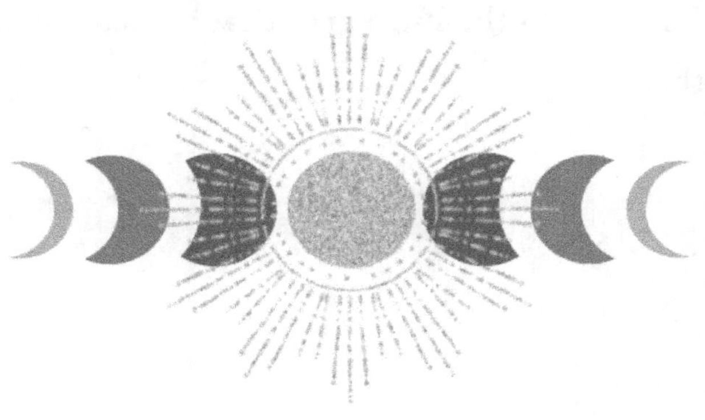

Chapter Fifteen

"Did you have fun with your sisters?" I ask as I shut the door to our bedroom. Reese spent a couple of hours talking to her sisters. Based on updates that my brothers received during their chat, they spent some time catching up but most of the time they were talking about us.

I do not mind. If talking to Ramsey and Rowan helped Reese get some of her questions answered, I am glad that she has them.

"Yes. I really needed to talk to them." Reese is wringing her hands in front of her, looking down at the floor shyly.

I walk over to her and tilt her chin so that she is looking at me. "You do not need to be nervous around me," I tell her.

She lets out a breath. "I know. I have just never done any of this before. I don't know what I am doing."

"I do not have any expectations. Tell me what you want. I will give you anything that you need."

She thinks for a little while, trying to work up the courage to voice what she wants.

"I know that it is late, but do you maybe want to take a bath with me?"

There's my brave girl.

"Of course," I tell her. We walk into the bathroom, and I begin filling the tub while she chooses different soaps and oils to add to the water.

"Is the vanilla part of your scent because of this soap or is it just you?"

I smile, a primal part of me likes that she has scented me. "I am not sure which came first. I have always liked that scent. It is actually similar to *your* scent."

"*My* scent? What do I smell like?" She adorably takes a sniff of her skin.

I stand close and bury my face in her neck. Fighting the urge to moan, I feel her shiver when my breath meets her skin. "You smell like cake, hot, right out of the oven."

"And you are cedar and vanilla tobacco." Her voice is raspy with desire. Her scent becomes thick with arousal. A low growl rumbles from my throat.

I slowly lift my shirt over her head, revealing her perfect body. My hands ghost down her sides before I reach for her hand and help her step into the water. Removing my pants, I lower myself into the bath behind her, cradling her in my arms.

She lets out a small gasp when she feels my cock rest against her ass.

"Just ignore that," I tell her. I do not want her to feel pressured in any way. But I also cannot hide my desire. Especially when we are sharing a bath.

We sat in comfortable silence for a little while. I wash our hair while she lathers our bodies with the vanilla soap. Her small hands are hesitant as she touches my heated skin.

"My sisters told me that Griff and War shave their legs for them. Would you, maybe, help me with that?"

I nod, not trusting my voice. I leave the tub and cross the room to locate the sharp knife that I use to shave my head.

Returning to the tub, I lower myself back into the water so that I am facing Reese. She reaches to hand me the soap, causing her dusky pink nipples to rise about the surface of the water. She must notice my attention, because her cheeks blush before she sinks back into the water.

"What did you talk to your sisters about," I ask as I begin sliding the sharp edge of the knife against her smooth skin.

"Um. You. Me."

"Us?" I smirk, enjoying how nervous she gets.

She nods. "I needed some advice."

"About us?" She nods again. "You can talk to me, you know."

I make quick work of her legs and then move to kneel in front of her, raising her arms to shave the underside of them like I know her sisters prefer. When I am done, I set the knife aside but do not move away.

"Kiss me." Her words leave her mouth so softly that I might have missed them altogether if I had not been so completely focused on her.

I pull her to me, one hand firm on her lower back, pressing her body flush to mine. My other hand gently cradles her face, and I crash my lips down to hers. She immediately opens for me, less hesitant than the first kiss we shared.

I have had previous bedmates, but I have never felt the desire to kiss anyone. It seemed too intimate for a quick fuck to satisfy a need.

But I could live off Reese's kisses. They are more vital to me than the air that I breathe. How I ever thought I could continue with my life without a Mate—without Reese—I will never understand. Now that I have had a taste, I want to taste every inch of her.

I may have a lot of sexual experiences under my belt, but just as Reese is untouched, I am finding that I have never experienced anything close to what it is like to be with her. My body is electrified wherever we touch. The glide of her skin against mine sparks pleasure so deep, I can feel it in my bones. Her taste is unlike anything that I have ever had before. It is exactly what I never knew I needed.

I swallow her moans as our tongues tangle with each other. My cock is painfully hard between us, weeping. With every swipe of her tongue against mine— every noise that she makes—I become closer and closer to completion.

I reach down and squeeze myself hard, needing to stop myself from shooting my seed all over her.

She begins grinding her perfect pussy against me, trying to find any relief from the burn she must be feeling.

"More," she pleads against my lips. I will give her anything. Everything. Hearing her beg makes my knot throb.

"Have you ever touched yourself, Wildflower?" I kiss down her neck, slowly moving down to pull her pebbled nipple into my mouth.

She nods and moans. "Only a few times."

I move my hand from her lower back down to her ass, squeezing the muscle.

"Can I taste you, sweetheart? Will you let me drown in your nectar?" I gently trail my finger over her slit.

"Yes," she says breathlessly.

She wraps her legs around my waist as I stand and carry her from the bathtub to our bed. There will be time for a frenzied counter or wall fuck later. This is her first time. I am going to take my time and make this perfect for her.

I lay her down on the bed, moving my body overtop of her as I take her mouth in a bruising kiss. When she rocks her hips up in search of me, I chuckle against her skin.

I work my lips down her body, paying extra attention to her nipples before swirling my tongue in her navel and placing kisses over her center.

"If you want me to stop, just say stop, okay?"

Reese nods and says, "I don't want you to stop. I want this. I *need* this."

I move my lips to the inside of her thighs, leaving small nips and kisses along her newly healed skin. Reese twines her fingers into my hair and moves my head over her center.

"Please, Bade."

My control snaps at the sound of her begging me and I devour her. My tongue flicks over her clit before diving into her folds. I work tight circles over her clit with my finger while my tongue fucks in and out of her, making her squirm and moan.

"Fuck, you taste delicious," I groan against her, unable to remove my lips from her. I need her taste like I need water. I don't want to drink anything else ever again.

"It feels...I have never felt so good," she tells me.

I can feel her walls fluttering around my tongue. She is so tight, I am going to need to stretch her before she is able to take my cock.

"Bade...I think..." and then she detonates. Her orgasm crashes through her as her body thrashes against my face. I need more.

I continue working her through the waves of her release before I slowly add one of my fingers. She is plenty wet, but she is so tight that it takes effort to slide it in all of the way. I climb myself back up her body as I gently move my finger.

"Taste how delicious you are." I kiss her and demand entry into her mouth. She opens immediately and sucks her arousal off of my tongue. The move pulls a moan from my mouth as jets of cum spray across the bedding.

"Fuck, sweetheart. You just made me come without even touching my cock."

"I did? Is...is that okay?" she asks shyly.

"You are perfect."

I move back down to her cunt and use my tongue to flick her clit while adding a second finger.

"Baby, I don't think that I can go again," she tells me. Her words are barely more than a gasp as she struggles to control her breathing. I moan at the new name she has assigned me.

Focusing my attention back on her, I increase the speed of my fingers as they glide in and out of her. "Yes, you can. You are going to give me one more. I can feel your pussy strangling my fingers. You are almost there already."

I curl my fingers and use my other hand to press down on her lower abdomen. She screams as she shatters, her arousal gushing out of her and soaking my hand.

"Good girl," I tell her as I slowly remove my fingers.

She gasps as she feels the loss of me. "How did you do that?" she asks. "I didn't know that it was possible to come more than once. I thought that only happened in books."

I smile and give her another kiss before climbing out of bed to retrieve a cloth to clean her up. She squirms as I take care of her.

"Don't get shy on me now," I tell her as her cheeks blush.

Reese crawls under the clean blanket that I put on the bed while she used the bathroom, not bothering to put any clothing on.

I join her moments later and pull her close. She sighs a contented sigh as she wiggles to use my arm as her pillow.

"Goodnight, Beast," she whispers.

I chuckle. "Sleep well, Wildflower."

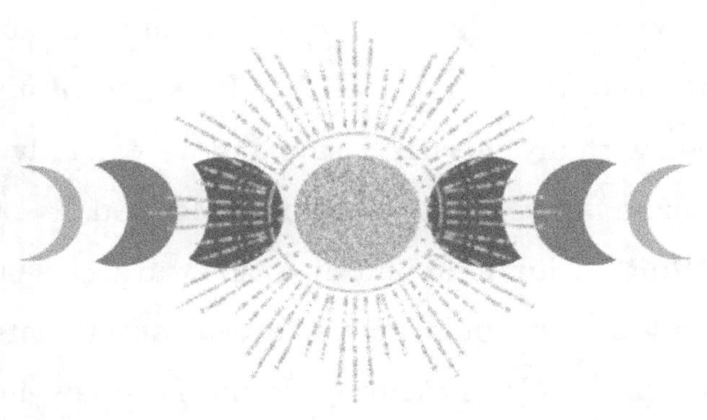

Chapter Sixteen

Reese

I wake up cocooned in warmth. Bade's body is completely entwined with mine. I turn in his arms and bury my face into his neck, breathing in his delicious scent. His hand gently runs down the length of my spine and over the curve of my ass before he hauls my leg up and over his hip.

"Why do you smell so good?" I ask, my voice is still raspy with sleep.

He chuckles. "We were made for each other, Wildflower. And *you* literally smell like dessert. How do you feel this morning?"

"Tired. A little sore. But really, really good."

"I would suggest that you sit on my face so that I can make you feel even better, but I just saw Juni crawl out of bed with my thermal vision and we will only have a minute or so before she comes looking for you."

"Shit!" I jump up and fly to the wardrobe, stealing one of Bade's shirts and throwing him a pair of pants while he laughs at me. "It's not funny! What if she saw us naked together?"

"She is a shifter, sweetheart. Nudity is normal. I do not think that she would think anything of it. But I agree that there are definitely some things that she shouldn't walk in on."

He is still laughing as I try to hurry him along with fastening his pants.

"Relax, love. We will teach her to knock. We will also speak to our siblings about making sure that the common rooms are off limits for certain activities."

Juni bursts through the door right as Bade playfully smacks my ass on his way to the bathroom.

"Good morning, honey, did you sleep okay?" I ask, still flustered.

"Yep! I had a dream where I was playing with Miss Ro's babies. We played hide and seek but they dinnit find me because I shifted and climbed up the tree."

I giggle with her. "That sounds fun! I'm sure you will get to play with them a lot after they are born."

"They called me cousin in my dream. Is that what I will be?"

"Yes, honey. They will be your cousins." I wrap her up in a big hug.

Bade walks out of the bathroom and ruffles Juni's hair in greeting. "Are you hungry, Princess?"

"That's why I found you, silly. My tummy is grumbly like an angry bear."

I quickly sneak off to the bathroom to relieve myself and brush my teeth before rejoining them. Bade throws Juni over his shoulder like a sack of potatoes and we head to the dining room.

Ramsey, Griffin, and Lycus are already there.

"Ro and War aren't early risers?" I ask as I give my sister a hug. Working as a barista in New York, Ro was always up before me.

Griffin snorts. "They have probably been up for a while already, but we will not see them for at least another hour."

Bade chuckles as he sets Juni down in the chair next to Ramsey. "What are you hungry for this morning?" he asks as he grabs a plate to start filling for her.

"Meat and fruit, please," she replies without even thinking about it.

"You got it." He sets her plate down in front of her and then fills a plate for me before making one for himself.

"What?" he asks when he notices everyone watching him, the tips of his ears pinking up.

"I've never seen you so domesticated," Griffin replies with a smirk.

"I'm just making sure my girls eat," Bade grumbles.

Ramsey mouths 'my girls, oh my god' to me as she holds her hand over her heart. I reach my hand under the table and give Bade's thigh a gentle squeeze. He puts his hand on mine and keeps it there for the rest of breakfast.

We are just cleaning up our plates when Ro and War walk in.

"Oh, man! We were trying to get here before you so that we could have breakfast with you on your first morning here, but I tried about six different outfits on before I finally found something that fits. I kept getting stuck in the outfits as I tried taking them back off, so War had to help me and that led to—"

"You don't need to complete that thought, Ro," I interrupt.

"Father, could you take Juni on a little walk in the garden? She had a dream last night that she was playing hide and seek in the garden with her cousins. Maybe she can show you the tree she climbed up in."

"Of course," Lycus says. "Maybe you can bring us some refreshments when you are done going over some new house rules with your brothers."

Lycus escorts Juni out of the room like the little queen that she is, giggling as they go.

Once they have left the room, I stand up and put on my serious face.

"Uh oh, Mom has her serious face on," Ro whispers across the table to Rams. "How did I get in trouble when I have only been here for a couple of minutes?"

"Juni is four...at least I think so." I turn to Bade, "We should probably figure that out somehow." Bade nods his agreement and I carry on. "Anyway, that's not the point right now. The point is that she is four, but she understands more than you think. Can we please try to be a little more aware of the words that are coming out of our mouths when she is in the room? Ro, I am mostly talking to you."

"Cross my heart," Ro replies with a giggle.

"And no fucking in the shared areas of the house," Bade adds.

Griffin and War both snort.

"What he means to say is that we are going to teach her to knock before entering a bedroom but if you could please keep it in your pants,"

"And wear pants," Bade interrupts.

"Yes, and *wear* pants around the shared parts of the house, we would really appreciate it."

"I'm sure that we can manage that," Ramsey replies for the group.

"Now that that is out of the way—and Juni is not in the room—I would like to know what you were up to last night about an hour after we left The Hideaway. Because War and I were up, walking a cramp out of my leg and I'm pretty sure I heard very not-sleep-like noises coming from your hallway," Ro says.

"Oh god!" I sink back down into my chair and cover my red face with my hands.

"'God' wasn't the name that I heard," she giggles.

"Ro, leave her alone," Ramsey scolds. "But come and get some tea from my stash later, okay?" she whispers to me across the table.

"Moving on... do you guys have any clothes that I can borrow until I get some for myself? Bade and I were going to take Juni shopping later, but I only have Bade's shirts to wear."

"Of course! You can raid our closets and take what you want," Ramsey tells me.

"War and I might join you, if that's okay? I need another dress or two to get me through this last month. I don't know how I could possibly grow any bigger and not tip over."

"You tipped over this morning," War teases under his breath.

"Maybe you should have held on a little tighter," she teases back, smacking him playfully on the arm.

"Maybe next time I will make you wait until *after* breakfast," he taunts jokingly.

Ro gasps. "Warrick Eugene Wolf, you will not deny me orgasms when you are the one who makes me this horny!"

War barks out a laugh. "That is definitely not my name."

"Well, I know that. But I needed to triple name you for emphasis and I just realized that we are Mated, married, about to have babies, and I don't even know your full name. Do we have a last name?"

"Yes, love," he says, still chuckling. "Our last name is Night."

"Huh, I never thought to ask either," Ramsey admits as Griffin laughs.

"That's two," he says to War and Bade as they both grumble.

"Two?" I ask, unsure what they are talking about.

"You had another bet going? What did you win this time?" Ramsey asks her Mate.

"Bragging rights, obviously."

"And?"

"And we get to have a date night where Bade and War have to serve us wearing clothing of our choosing!"

The room fills with a mixture of laughter and groans as the full terms of this bet come to light.

"So, we are Nights now?" Ro asks after Griffin and Ramsey's maniacal laughter dies down.

"Yeah. What was your family name back in New York?" War asks.

"Hunt. I was Rowan Kate Hunt."

"And I was Ramsey Grace Hunt."

I turn to look at Bade as I add, "And I am Reese Josephine Hunt."

"Not for long," he replies under his breath. My stomach flutters at his mumbled words.

Bade slings his arm around my shoulders and pulls me in close. "Why don't you go steal some clothes from your sisters and I will steal any books that Griff has about bear-shifters. We can all have lunch at the market."

"That sounds like a perfect plan." I lean in and press a quick kiss to his lips.

"We can stop in the garden on the way. I will give Juni a little spa moment while you try on some clothes," Ramsey says.

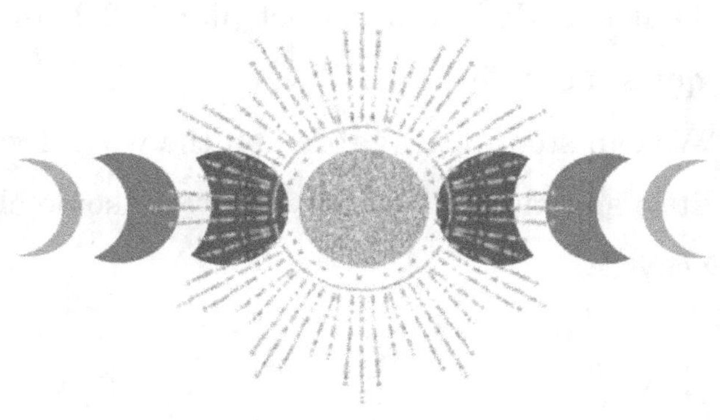

Chapter Seventeen

"I already have some books about non-wolf shifters pulled but there should be more on that shelf over there," Griff says as he points me towards a shelf across the room.

I head over to the shelf while he starts sorting through the books already on his desk.

"Any that are on bears specifically have a sun on the spine, but there are more that discuss a variety of shifter species as well," Griff adds.

I pull four books off the shelf that have suns on the spines and add them to the pile that Griff is compiling.

War has already taken a seat and is flipping through one.

"Thank you for helping me with this," I tell them. "Now that we know Juni is having visions like Reese, we want to prepare as much as we can."

"I never would have guessed that you would be the first to have a pup—or cub," War admits.

"Me either," I confess. "I do not know how to explain it but after Reese told me about her, I could feel that she was meant to be ours just as much as Reese is mine."

"It is fated," Griff says with a shrug.

"Now I just need to get Reese to agree to a bonding ceremony."

"You don't think that she will agree?" Griff asks.

I sigh. "I completely fucked everything up in the beginning."

"Bade told her that he did not want a Mate," War shares.

Griff snorts. "You cannot ignore a True Mate bond. Why would you try?"

"You saw what happened to our father. I cannot lose her. I would not survive it." Being vulnerable in front of anyone like this is not something that I am used to. I do not usually share my feelings with anyone. But because of Reese, I am starting to see that it is okay to share—maybe even necessary.

"I have a feeling these Hunt women are more resilient than they appear at first glance," Griff smiles, probably thinking about the strength of his own Mate, who has overcome so much since coming to this world.

The strength of our Mates is something we can all agree on.

Griff, War, and I stay in the library for the rest of the morning. I found a book on legends that discusses the creation and Sun Kissed origins.

Like the wolves, the bears believe in The Mother. She is the creator of all life. Wolves believe that The Moon is the Mate of The Mother and has therefore extended additional blessings to some True Mate pairs. Moon Touched.

Bears believe that The Sun is the sister to The Mother. The Sun helps support the life that The Mother has created and has similarly extended additional blessings to certain bears that will help The Mother in extraordinary ways. I re-read the passage several times to commit it to memory.

"I do not think that being Sun Kissed is connected to Mates at all." Flipping back and forth between the pages I just found, I continue, "It seems more of a familial link, passed down through the females in their line. It would explain why Sylas does not have a marking.

Though, Juni does not have one yet either. Maybe the trigger is something different than it was for us?"

I show the passage to Griff and War.

"That could be," Griff agrees. "Her Nana had the same powers, right?"

"Yeah. Juni calls her a daydreamer." It is fucking adorable.

I keep reading. A lot of the passage discusses clan dynamics. While it is interesting, I mostly skim over that information for now. She will be living in a pack for possibly her entire life. We can learn more about clans later.

"I found something else," I tell my brothers as I show them the passage.

And on the eve of their fifth birthday,
The Sun will shine down
and bestow a kiss upon the Blessed
Forever marking her a Sister of The Mother

"Do we know when her birthday is?" War asks.

"No. Reese told me that she is four, but I do not know if Juni even knows. She lived on her own for a while before she found Reese."

"Well, I guess we will find out when she gets her mark. Since she does not have one yet, we know that she

157

is younger than five. Bear shifters are bigger than wolves as adults, but she seems smaller than wolves that are her age, doesn't she?" Griff asks.

War and I both agree—though we are certainly not experts on the matter.

Before we know it, the ladies find us for lunch. We all head out together, weaving through the market in Nighthowl. Juni pulls us from stall to stall, her eyes sparkling with wonder as she sees a variety of things for the first time.

When we enter the shop of the clothier that Rowan and Ramsey have used before, he wastes no time taking measurements for both Reese and Juni and adjusting a few already made pieces to send home with us today.

I have never really cared about shopping but watching how Reese and Juni light up when they find something that they like settles another piece of my soul.

While Reese pulls Juni into a soapery with her sisters, War and I sneak off to the jeweler that Griff recommended. At their bonding ceremony, Griff gave Ramsey a ring as a physical reminder of their commitment to each other. It is something that is done in their world. Wanting something similar for Rowan and Reese, we work with the jeweler to customize pieces. And, because my heart has also been stolen by a special little girl, I ask the jeweler to make a coordinating piece for her too.

By the time we are done at the jeweler, everyone is ready to head back to the lodge. Juni begins to fall asleep snuggled up against Reese's chest, so I carefully pull her into my arms and carry her back. I cannot help but chuckle when her little snores fill my ears.

A few days later, Rowan and Ramsey get called out to a delivery. The mother, Eden, is one of the females who became pregnant once Rowan received her magic. She and her True Mate, Arlo, already have two children and are now expecting twins.

With most of the family out of the house for the night, I arrange a surprise for Reese after we tuck Juni into bed.

"It is beautiful out here," she tells me as I lead her into the garden. Candles and bright flowers decorate the space when I have a late dinner waiting for us.

"I thought that we could spend time getting to know each other better. I know that we did not have the best start."

"I have already forgiven you for that," she tells me quietly. "I understand why you tried to push me away."

"I wish that I would not have."

"Thank you for all of this." She waves her hand around in an excited flurry. "I have never been on a date before." Neither have I.

"What was it like back in your world?"

"Loud," she laughs. "And busy. And expensive. But Ramsey always made sure that we had what we needed. I was attending school to become a teacher. I always wanted to help children. In the summers, I taught swim lessons and worked as a lifeguard at a neighborhood pool."

"You like to swim?"

"Yeah. I love it actually. One of the families that I stayed with for over a year had a cabin that they used in the warmer months. Being at the lake made me realize how much I loved being in nature. Living in a city as big as New York, well, it's easy to forget how calming being away from it all can be." As she speaks, my attention zeros in on her lips.

"Can I kiss you?" We have shared many since our first kiss a week ago, but I will never get enough.

"Yes, please." Her eyes heat as her breathing becomes heavy with anticipation.

I grip her chair and slide it close. Gently holding her face in my hands, I press my lips to her. With this kiss, I want to tell her what my words fail to say. That she is everything to me. That she has my heart and my soul. That I want this with her—all of it—for this lifetime and the next. That I am so fucking sorry for any pain or heartbreak that she experienced—whether I was the cause or not. I know that her life before she came here was not an easy one. But she still found the positives. Despite her circumstances, she came out on the other side as one of the strongest people I have ever known.

I kiss her until we are both breathless. Then, I slowly pull away. "Thank you for not giving up on me."

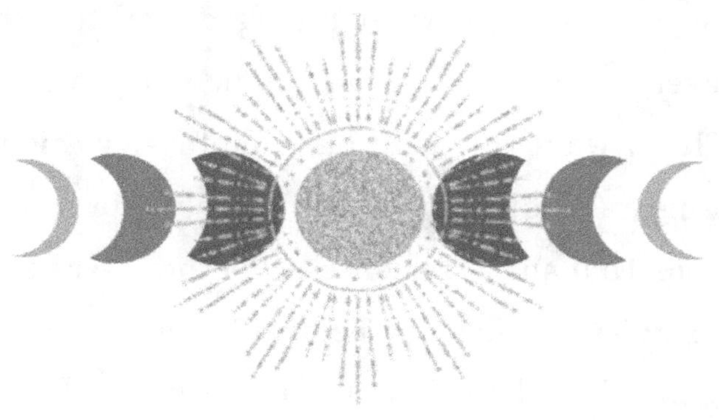

Chapter Eighteen

Reese

After dinner, Bade and I return to our room. Using some of the soaps that we picked up at the market this week, he fills the tub full of steamy water and delicious smelling bubbles. Kissing me again, he slowly strips me of my clothes as I reach for the ties of his pants.

Bade never wears a shirt. It is actually funny to me that he even owns any. His tan, tattooed skin is still warm from the summer day as I trail my fingers over his hard muscles.

"I want to learn every inch of your body," he says against my skin as he kisses my neck, flicking his tongue over my pulse point in a way that sends liquid heat rushing to my core.

He lifts me up and steps into the bathtub with me, lowering us together so that I am straddling his lap. The motion presses his hard cock against my clit, relieving some of the pressure that is already building.

"I want it all," he continues. "Everything. I want the life with you that I know we are destined to have."

I pull his lips back to mine, allowing him to swallow my moans as our tongues twine. As I bring my hands up and gently hold the sides of his face, my vision shines silver.

I walk through the forest with only the light of the moon showing the way. Next to me, Juni holds my hand, wearing a dress made of pretty flowers. My body is bare, aside from jeweled cuffs and a crown made of wildflowers.

We walk until we reach a lake. Bade stands at the shore under an arch of flowers. On either side of the aisle, our family sits with smiles on their faces. Ramsey scoops Juni onto her lap as I continue on to stand with my Mate.

I gasp as the vision fades.

"Are you okay, Wildflower?"

"Yes," I tell him. "I just had a vision of us. I think it was our bonding ceremony."

Bade's eyes soften. "What did you see?"

"We were at a lake. There were flowers everywhere. Our family was there, and we were bare ass naked," I say with a giggle.

He chuckles. "That was definitely our bonding ceremony. Do you know when it will happen?" His words are quiet but hopeful.

I shake my head. "It was warm out. Ro and War were holding their babies and Juni had a gold sun on her temple. Not the full moon tomorrow but maybe the next? Or the one after that? Is that too soon? I don't want to pressure you into it."

"Sweetheart, I would bond with you right now if it was possible. I love you. And I love our little girl. I was serious when I said that I wanted it all. I want the family, the babies, the chaos, the adventures." Bade buries his face in my neck. "I want all of your days and all of your nights."

"I want that too." I admit. "It is all I have ever wanted. Do you remember when you asked me why I was still a virgin, and I told you that it didn't matter anymore? It is because I always knew that I only wanted to share that part of myself with you. Even when I was worlds away, I always knew that everything that I am, every part of me, belonged with you—to you. Just as much as I knew that you belonged to me—with me. Even when I only knew you in my dreams.”

Bade’s mouth crashes down on mine, bruising my lips. I follow his lead. I would never deny him; I *could* never deny him. He owns me completely, mind, body, and soul.

Lifting me out of the bathtub, Bade carries me into our bedroom, kissing me the entire way. Positioning me on the edge of the bed, he drops to his knees and licks me ass to clit in one hard stroke.

“Fucking delicious,” he says as he continues to work me over with his tongue. I squirm beneath him, my thighs locking around his head as he sucks hard on my clit. He growls against my skin and pushes my legs wider, holding my thighs against the mattress. The image of being bared so completely to him—he can see *every* part of me—makes fire blaze a path through my center. I am so completely turned on right now, a light breeze could probably make me come.

He alternates between pushing his tongue in and out of my channel and flicking my clit, building my climax higher and higher until I combust. I cry out his name as my vision blacks out and I see stars.

“Good girl,” he tells me as I moan through the release.

I feel so full as Bade pushes one of his large fingers into my pussy. "Oh god," I gasp. "How am I going to fit your huge cock when I feel so full with just a finger?"

He laughs against my thigh, sucking and nipping as he works his way back to my clit. "We will go slow. But first, you are going to let my fingers stretch you out."

Bade works his finger in and out at a slow and steady pace, adding another finger, and then curling and scissoring until he makes room for a third. It is the best kind of uncomfortable as I near the edge of another release.

He works his tongue up my body, tugging on and flicking my hard nipples.

"That's it, Wildflower. I can feel your walls trying to milk my fingers. Come all over my hand and then you can milk my cock."

His dirty words push me over the edge; my body convulses as my orgasm crashes through me. Bade brings his fingers to his mouth, licking them clean before kissing me fiercely. I moan at the taste of myself on his tongue.

Lining up the head of his cock to my entrance, Bade pauses. I realize that he is giving me a chance to stop.

"Please, baby," I beg, "I want to feel you. I am ready."

"I will go slow. If you need me to stop, just say stop, okay?"

"Okay," I nod.

"You might feel a pinch of pain when I break through. You will probably bleed. But I promise I will make you feel so good, sweetheart."

"I trust you." I reach down and hold him to my pussy as he begins pushing inside. He goes slow, just like he promised, allowing me time to adjust.

Reaching between us, Bade works gentle circles over my clit, encouraging me to relax as he moves a little more.

"You are doing so well," he tells me. I preen under his praise which allows him in a little more.

I gasp as a twinge of pain brings a few tears to my eyes. Bade swipes them away with his thumbs, a flash of concern on his face.

"I'm okay. Keep talking. It helps."

His blue eyes darken to navy and a seductive smirk tugs at the corner of his mouth. "Does my Mate like to hear dirty words? Are you going to take my big cock into your tight virgin hole?"

"Yes," I rasp out. "So full."

Bade peppers kisses all over my chest and neck. "We are about halfway there, sweetheart. You are taking me so well."

I pull his lips to meet mine, needing the distraction from the discomfort as my body adjusts to fit him. Little by little, Bade works his cock further into my body until finally, I can feel a massive bulge press against my clit.

"What is that?" I ask, shocked, as I reach between us to feel it with my hand.

Bade groans as my fingers make contact.

"My knot," he explains. "Did your sisters not tell you?"

Like in the omegaverse books that I read back in New York? Apparently, my sisters left some vital information out when they told me that he would fit.

"I don't think…there isn't room," I pant out, nervous that he might try making that fit too, but so close to coming again that I don't want him to stop. Feeling his knot rubbing against my clit almost pushes me over the edge.

"You will not have my knot this time. We will work up to it, okay love?"

I nod. Unable to form words as my walls flutter around him.

Bade pulls his cock out until just his head remains and then firmly but slowly pushes back in. I gasp as he hits places inside of me that I didn't even know existed. He fucks me in a steady rhythm that causes me to melt into him. I am a puddle of pure pleasure as he gently builds my orgasm into something so intense that it steals my breath. It is unlike anything that I have ever felt before.

"Breathe, sweetheart," he whispers into my ear—our sweat mixing as he presses his forehead against my neck.

"Baby, I need…"

"I know, Wildflower. I know what you need."

He reaches between us, working my clit as his thrusts speed up. He drags his teeth down my neck on the way to my breasts before clamping down hard on my nipple with his teeth, pinching the other with his free hand.

I scream. My release rockets out of me and the world around us completely fades. It is just Bade and me, floating in outer space. Sweating, writhing, being shattered apart and made new–together. Bade roars his own release seconds later as his cum shoots deep inside me.

We stay connected, catching our breath for a while. It could have been a minute or a year—all I know is the feel of Bade's heart beating as if it might come out of his chest.

"Are you okay?" he asks as he wipes the tears I didn't know I shed from my cheeks.

"Yes," I tell him with a kiss on his lips. "That was so intense. So perfect."

"It has never been like that before," he admits.

Bade rolls so that he is on his back and I am draped over him. My entire body feels like jelly, and I can still feel my inner walls clamping down on him.

"Are you sore?" he asks, pressing a kiss to my damp forehead.

"Yes," I wince. "A little. But I like it," I admit as I press my face into the crook of his neck, breathing in his delicious scent. We lay together for a while, content to just breathe the same air, holding each other tightly.

I must have fallen asleep because I am woken up near orgasm, Bade's tongue lapping at my center in soothing strokes. He moans at the taste of me—the taste of us, I realize. Seeing that I am awake, he thrusts his tongue deep. I am so close.

"Please," I beg. I don't even know what I need but he does. He rises from between my legs to bring his mouth level with mine.

"Taste," he growls before spitting our mixed release into my mouth. The filthiness of the act pushes me straight over the edge. My inner walls squeeze around his cock as he thrusts deeply back inside me, filling me again.

"Go back to sleep, Wildflower. Sleep with your pussy strangling my cock. Now that I have found my home, you will never feel empty again."

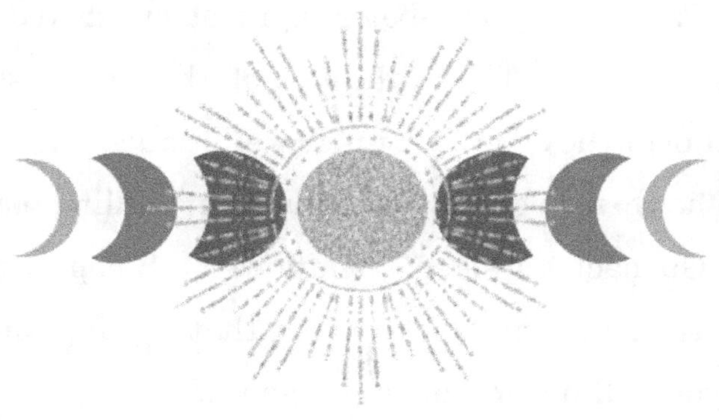

Chapter Nineteen

Reese wakes slowly the next morning. I snuck out of bed earlier to make a tray of breakfast for us to share. She is going to need to refuel her body after last night. I took her four more times during the night, unable to resist filling her. I made sure to use my tongue each time, hoping that my saliva would help heal any soreness that she would normally feel.

On my way to grab breakfast, I made arrangements for Juni to spend the morning with Griff and Ramsey. Luckily, she had already made her way to the dining room without first coming to our room. I told her that Reese was feeling tired this morning, and she was content with getting a quick snuggle from me before turning her attention back to her plate of pancakes.

"Good morning, Beast," Reese says with a smile as she rolls her body closer to me. I press a kiss to her lips, rewarding her with my mouth and releasing a satisfied growl as she works her tongue against mine. My cock pulses with the need to be back inside of her but I hold myself back since I know she must still be a little sore.

"Did you sleep well?" I ask her against her lips.

"Mhmm." She yawns. "I had this amazing dream where I woke up orgasming over and over and over again."

I chuckle. "That sounds like a great dream. The reality was just as delicious."

"If I knew *sleeping* with you would have been like that from the beginning, I might not have worked so hard at finding somewhere else to lay down for the night." She giggles and the sound wraps itself around my heart.

"I have never actually *slept* with another before you," I admit.

"Seriously? I just assumed that you have had many lovers before me."

"Fucking does not require sleeping together. It always seemed too personal to stay after. Same as kissing. That rarely happened. And I have never tasted another before. Only you. It is completely new and different with you. Even when I was in denial, I still needed you in my bed. That is why I moved you back every night."

"I never want to sleep without you again." She presses a gentle kiss to my lips. It is quick, casual, as if we have been kissing each other for our whole lives already. "Do I smell pancakes?" Her stomach rumbles, making me bark out a laugh.

As Reese eats, I run us a bath. While I would love for her to keep smelling so strongly of me, I know that she will feel more comfortable after a relaxing soak.

An hour later, we are both fed, clean, and dressed and emerge from our room in search of our family. We find them all in the garden. We watch as Juni shouts out a color for Rowan and then squeals in delight as Ro makes a flower of that color sprout up from the soil.

War is sitting nearby with Sylas as they discuss hunting routes.

Ramsey and Griffin are sprawled out on a blanket under a shady tree reading.

Life at the lodge has changed so drastically in the last few months, it is a stark contrast to how it once was. I cannot help but think that *this* is how it was always supposed to be. How my mother would have wanted it to be.

When she sees us approach, Juni runs towards us, hugging our legs. We both sink to our knees to be on her level and pull her into our arms.

"Are you having fun, honey bear?" Reese asks her.

"So much! Auntie Ro is makin' flowers grow. She made me a crown out of them to play princess."

"Can you make me one too?" Reese asks.

Juni nods. "I was going to bring you some if you were still sleeping. Bade told me that you needed to sleep even though it was already day."

"Thank you for letting me sleep in. I did not sleep very much last night."

"Did you have real dreams too? I had a real dream about making flower crowns."

"Does that happen a lot?" I ask Juni. It seems like she has visions more often than Reese does. Since we believe she is nearing her 5th birthday, it is possible that her powers are becoming stronger.

"I think so. Sometimes I can't tell. But this was in my real dream last night. It is just the same." She leans in close to whisper, "Watch Uncle Griff." We turn to look at Griff for a few moments before a nut falls from the tree and bounces off of his head. He curses while Ramsey giggles. Juni is giggling too.

"Thanks for the warning, Princess," Griff chuckles with us once he realizes what happened.

"Juni, do you remember when your birthday is? Did you celebrate it with your Nana?" Reese asks.

"It's the day with the long, bright sun. Nana said that the day is longer so that we have more time to have fun," she says with a smile.

"That is in a few days. The solstice marks the longest day of sun during the warmer months," I say.

"What should we do to celebrate?" Reese asks.

"We already know, silly. We go swimmin' at the lake and then have roast and cake before Auntie Ro has her babies." Juni must notice that all of us are staring at her, surprised by the news she just shared. "Oops. Nana told me sometimes dreams need to stay in our heads. Was that one of them?" Worry flashes through her eyes, thinking that she did something wrong.

"No, Princess. You can always tell us," I reassure her.

"Thank god!" Rowan shouts. "Don't get me wrong, I have loved being pregnant. But I am so ready to be done. War, let's go. We need to get their room finished before I start popping them out." War shakes his head, laughing, as he follows her inside.

"Well, it sounds like we have a party to plan," Reese says as she reaches for Juni's hand and walks with her over to the blanket Ramsey is stretched out on.

I take War's vacated seat next to Sylas. "How have you been? Has the transition to being in the village worked out okay for you?"

"Yeah. War put me on Arlo's routes so that he can take some time off now that their twins are here. It is a miracle that multiples are surviving again."

"Thank The Mother and The Moon."

We sit quietly together for a little while longer before Sylas excuses himself and returns to his home and I join my girls under the tree.

Placing a lopsided flower crown on my head, Juni giggles and climbs into my lap. "Reese says that men can wear flower crowns too."

"Did you make this?" She nods shyly. "Then I will wear it with pride." I tickle her before we decide to team up and tickle Reese instead.

After we are all tired from laughing, we settle in while Griff begins reading his book out loud. Reese and Juni both fall asleep while using me as a pillow. I look over to my brother to see Ramsey asleep as well.

"How did we get so lucky?" I ask him quietly.

"I do not know. But I am thankful every day for it," he replies. "Things are going well with Reese, then?"

"More than. I did not realize that things would be this…intense…before the bonding ceremony. I always thought that the *need* was due to the after-bond heat."

"It will always be intense," he tells me, "But with time it will even out a bit. The bond will help settle it."

Juni is sound asleep and snoring, but I cover her ears anyway.

"I made Reese sleep impaled on my cock last night," I whisper to him. "I do not know if that is normal but, fuck, I never want to sleep any differently again."

"I didn't need to know that," Ramsey mumbles, half asleep as Griff works hard to quiet his laugh.

Switching to talk mind to mind, I ask, *"Seriously, though, is it normal? I have done some kinky shit over the years, but nothing has ever come close to this need to fill her."*

"If Ramsey ever finds out that I told you this, I will castrate you, but she currently has a butt plug shoved up her ass holding my seed in. Clearly, I might not be the best one to ask about what is 'normal' behavior with your Mate but as long as you are both okay with it, I say, go for it."

"Fuck, I need one of those. Here I thought you were the tame one out of us three."

"Any updates on Briggs?" he asks out loud.

"Boone spoke to a bear scout from a border clan. They have not seen Briggs at all. It is possible he stayed under radar and moved into a different territory, but nobody has had eyes on him since he escaped the night that I found Reese."

Griff curses under his breath. "Hopefully he stays gone."

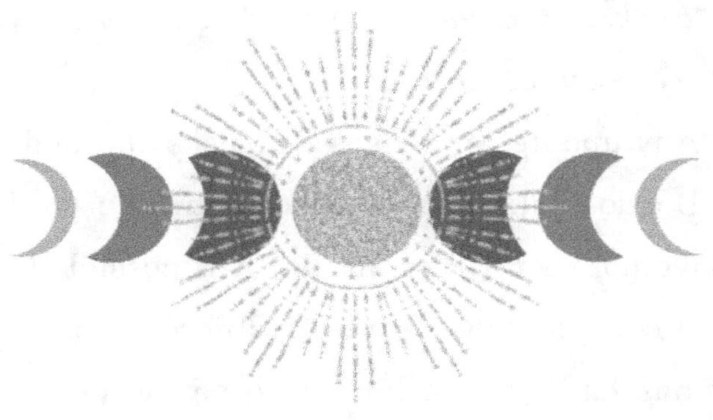

Chapter Twenty

The day before Juni's birthday, the lodge is in chaos. In the last two days, we helped War and Ro with their nursery, shopped for gifts for both Juni and the babies, and have scoured all of the books Griffin has in his library to learn about bear shifters and what we should expect to happen when Juni receives her full powers.

In addition to all of that, there were four births that Heka and Ramsey have been called out on. Ro was insistent that she should be allowed to go as well, but finally gave in to War's demands that she stays at the lodge and rest before their babies arrive. Although she may have agreed to stay at the lodge, she is a bit grumpy about it.

"Want to help me make Juni's birthday cake?" I ask her as I enter the kitchen.

"You want me to help you?" she asks with a bit of sass in her tone. "Me? The person who cannot even boil water?"

I chuckle. "I was mostly wondering if you could help find and read the recipe. Bade told me that his mother's birthday cake recipe is in this book. I was going to have him translate it for me but since you are here…"

"Okay. But you need to help distract me from the fact that I am going to have to push three babies out of my cooch tomorrow night."

I snort. "We can talk about anything you want as long as we get the cake made."

"Anything?" She waggles her eyebrows at me. Both of my sisters have been trying to get details about my now blooming love life, though Ramsey is much more subtle about it than Ro is.

Groaning, I nod. I know that look in her eye. I can already feel my cheeks heat. Ramsey walks in looking completely exhausted as she heads straight to the fridge and pulls out a tray of food. She eats half of it before looking up to acknowledge us.

"Oh, hey."

"Oh, hey," Ro replies. "How did it go?"

"Fine. Twins. No issues other than the father passing out when he took a look mid-push. Who knew wolves could be so squeamish?"

Ro and I both laugh.

"Are there any more due, other than Ro, of course?" I ask.

"Hey! Talking about it is not a good way to distract me," Ro whines.

"No others. At least, not that we know of. There is always the chance that someone delivers early."

"Want to help us make Juni's cake?"

"Of course. What recipe are we using? Griffin has been teaching me to cook a bit but some of the ingredients are completely different from what we are used to." She looks at the book in front of Ro, nodding as she reads off the ingredients.

"It is so strange to me that you can read this. It just looks like random symbols to me."

"That will change once you are Mated. When will that be? Have you forgiven him for being an asshat yet?" Ro asks.

"I forgave him right away, if I'm honest. I understand why he tried to fight it. The situation with his parents really messed with his head."

"He never should have rejected you, though," Ro grumbles.

Ro is right. He shouldn't have pushed me away. But she is also wrong. "He never actually rejected me," I defend. "His words hurt but they were honest. And he may have tried to push me away, but he also brought me back to his room every night and then slept on the floor outside the door. He was warring with himself more than with me."

"Regardless, it is clear that he wants this with you now," Ramsey says as she grabs the ingredients that we will need for the cake as we chat.

"Yeah. He wants it all. I was worried that it might be too much—that adding Juni into the mix would be a lot. Especially since he was hesitant about me in the beginning. But you have seen how he is with her. She is just as much his little girl as she is mine."

"And you want it all too?" Ramsey asks.

I nod. "I love him," I admit quietly. "I haven't told him that yet though. It seems like everything is just happening so fast. I mean, I have never been in a relationship before. Is it too fast?"

Ramsey and Rowan give each other a look before Rowan says, "Everything is faster here. The True Mate soul thing speeds it all up. I barely even knew War before he was making me come all over his face. It just felt right with him from the beginning."

"It was different with Griffin. But that was because I had trauma that I needed to deal with. I always felt comfortable with him, though, even when I couldn't be in the same room as another man," Ramsey adds as a small smile tugs at her lips.

Ramsey has come so far since she first arrived. She had shared her experiences with me when I first came to the lodge. She needed to make sure that I did not suffer in the same way. The guilt that she felt over trusting the person who drugged us at the club was still eating away at her. When I told her that a friend from school helped keep me safe that night, we sobbed in each other's arms. Ramsey cried because she was grateful. I cried because I was heartbroken by what she endured.

"He told me that he loves me. And Juni. He has been completely open with me ever since he apologized on our way to pick up Juni. Long gone is the beast who growled more than he talked, though I still call him one."

"Oh, I met him when I first came here," Ro says. "He was a man of few words—mostly grumbles, grunts, and sharp one-liners. But he is different now that he has you and Juni. It is like you not only hold his soul, but you also have the magical communication chip that he needed in order to function as a real human…er…wolf.”

He definitely knows how to use his words now. My face heats as I remember the way his dirty mouth brought me to orgasm.

“I had a vision of our bonding. We are going to bond at the next moon.” I am hopeful that this announcement will steer this conversation, and my thoughts, back into a safe territory. Otherwise, I am going to have to track down Bade and have him use his words again.

Rowan squeals and Ramsey smiles as they both wrap me up in a hug.

“So,” Ro says, “what is the kinkiest thing you have done so far?”

Or, not. When I shoot her a look of surprise at her question, she giggles.

“You said that we could talk about *anything* while we make this cake.”

I roll my eyes as I try to come up with the right answer. Other than his mouth, there is really only one thing that would qualify as ‘kinky’. But I can’t share that…right? Ugh.

"I'm not sure. He is mostly really gentle and sweet with me." It isn't a lie. He is incredibly gentle with me in and out of the bedroom.

"That's not what I heard," Ramsey mumbles.

"What?! What have you heard?" I panic. How has she heard? She can't know…right?

"I knew it!" Ro says as she holds her belly to laugh. "All of the Night brothers are filthy. Even golden retriever Griff is freaky in the sheets." Ramsey's blush confirms it.

"What do you mean? I'm pretty sure that what we have done is pretty tame—other than me sleeping with him inside of me. Bade would tell me if he needed more, right?"

"Ooh, I fall asleep on War's knot sometimes too."

"He hasn't knotted me," I confess, feeling more and more self-conscious that I am not doing this right. "He just stays inside me all night long. It has only been a few days, but I honestly don't know if I could fall asleep without him anymore."

"Fuck, that's hot," Ro says under her breath. Ramsey smacks her playfully on the arm. "What? It's the baby hormones. I can't help it."

"Just for the record, that *is* kinky," Ramsey says. "As far as whether or not Bade needs 'more', there is no way that he isn't fully satisfied. I'm sure that if there are more things that he is into or would like to try with you, he will communicate that. He is probably just taking things slow since this is all new to you."

"More things like what?" We place the cake in the oven and set the timer.

"Oral, anal, spanking, choking, dirty talk, bondage, blindfolds, getting it on in public..." Ro continues naming things, and my mind is going haywire. I don't even know what I would like but it all sounds intriguing to me. I used to read romance books back in New York and the spicy scenes always got to me. Maybe I should make a list of things to try. Is that weird?

"It isn't weird if you are both into it," Ro replies. I didn't realize I asked that out loud. What if I'm not enough? What if he just isn't telling me that he needs more because he is worried that I can't handle it? I know that he said that it is different with me. And that there are things that he does with me that he hasn't done before–like eating me out–but what if he isn't getting everything that he needs?

"Just talk to him, Reese. He will be honest with you," Ramsey says as she pulls me into another hug.

My sisters continue talking while I mix up some frosting, lost in thought. Once the cakes are out and cool, Ro grows some edible flowers, and Ramsey helps me decorate the cake to look like the sun.

After we clean up, we meet the guys in the library. Bade is sitting with Juni on his lap, helping her read a children's book. Not wanting to interrupt them, I stay near the doorway, watching as my heart flutters in my chest. He is so amazing with her. Not once has he ever shown any hesitation towards caring and providing for her.

Knowing that I am there, Bade looks up and winks at me. When their book is finished, Ramsey offers to take Juni outside to play. Juni gives me a hug before taking Ramsey's hand and leading her outside.

I walk over to Bade and crawl into his lap, sealing my lips to his in a bruising kiss. Completely forgetting that we are not alone, I grind my pussy against his hardening cock, making him moan.

I distantly hear Rowan giggle before Bade pulls his mouth from mine to say, "Lock the door on your way out." War snorts and then the door closes. As soon as the door clicks shut, Bade pulls my dress up over my head, leaving me completely bare for him.

"Fuck, Wildflower. I could scent your arousal as soon as you walked in the door. Feeling needy, sweetheart?"

"Mmhmmm," I moan. "I need you."

Bade wastes no time as he stands, holding me to his body as I continue to grind myself against him. He props me up against a bookshelf.

"Do you need my fingers, mouth, or cock, love?"

Feeling confident, I tell him exactly what I want. "I need your cock hard and fast…and then your mouth nice and slow."

"Good girl," he growls as he rids himself of his pants, sliding into me in one hard stroke. Bade thrusts in and out of me just as I asked. He holds the back of my head to make sure that I don't hit it against the wood of the bookshelf as he fucks me hard. There is no controlling the sounds that are coming out of my mouth. The bite of the wood behind my back only adds to the pleasure of Bade's giant cock hitting all of the right places inside me. I can feel his swollen knot against my clit, sometimes touching, teasing the rim of my ass while Bade shifts positions slightly.

Leaning his head down, he pulls my nipple into his mouth, flicking the sensitive bud before moving over to the other. Just when I think he is going to tease me there too, he bites down. Hard. I scream as my release barrels through me, wave after wave.

"Fuck, your greedy pussy is milking me so good, taking all of my seed. I want to fill you up so full. See you swell with my pups. Do you want that too, Wildflower?"

"Yes," I moan. His words stretch out my orgasm.

"Take. It. All," he says as his thrusts become wild and he pours himself into my pulsing heat.

Still inside me, Bade carries me over to an empty table and lays me down. Pulling out, he pushes his release back into my body with his fingers.

"You look so good with your cunt swollen and messy." His voice is gravelly with desire.

"Maybe you should clean me up," I boldly tell him.

"Hands and knees," he commands, pulling out the chair to sit behind me. I quickly follow his directions. Pulling me to his face, he runs his nose through my slit. "You smell so fucking delicious." His tongue is next, licking from my clit all the way up to my ass. I moan as his tongue circles my most intimate places.

Bade hums against my skin. "You like that? Will you let me claim this hole too? I want all of your pretty holes."

"Please," I beg and push my ass back into his face.

He chuckles. "So greedy." He swipes his thumb through my folds before pressing it gently against my back hole. The moan that leaves my mouth is almost feral. "Interesting," he says.

"Please, baby. I need it."

"What do you need, sweetheart? My finger or my tongue."

"Your tongue." The words are barely out before Bade spreads my cheeks wide and dives in. His tongue soaks the ring of my asshole, alternating between flicks and pressure.

"Fuuuuuuuck," the word leaves me through my chest. I have never felt anything like this before. My release starts to build. An intense heat rising in my core. Bade pushes his tongue into me, gently fucking in and out.

Pulling away, he bites my ass cheek. "You are such a good girl, taking my tongue in your ass." He continues to build my orgasm with his tongue, plunging it into me as deep as it can go, until I shatter. His tongue is still inside me as my entire body convulses and my vision goes dark. It isn't until after the intensity recedes that I notice how wet the table is beneath me.

"Did you come too?" I ask, still dazed.

Bade chuckles. "Yes. But *that* was all you."

I look closer to see that his hand is still holding his cock, covered in his own release while mine is pooling on the table.

"Did I...is that normal?" The amount of liquid pooling beneath me seems impossible.

"Yes, sweetheart. It might not happen every time, but it is normal," he reassures me. "It just tells me that you really enjoy anal. You really are perfect for me." Bade takes my mouth in a kiss so fierce that it marks my soul, alleviating some of my worry.

Lifting me off of the table, he holds me to his body as he sinks back down in the chair. I look around the space and see the damage we did to the place. Books have fallen off of the shelf he fucked me against. The table is dripping. Papers are scattered on the floor.

"We should probably clean this up before Griffin finds out what we just did in his library."

Bade throws his head back and laughs. "Wildflower, with his sensitive sense of smell, no amount of cleaning is going to hide this from him. He will be smelling us for weeks."

My face flames red.

"If it makes you feel any better, I can guarantee that this is not the only action these books have been witness to."

"Ew," I say with a chuckle as I bury my head against Bade's neck.

After a few quiet moments, Bade shifts me so that he can see my face. "Are you okay? I know that was different from what we have done before. And the pups thing, I probably should not have brought that up mid thrust."

I start to panic. Is he regretting it? Was it just something said in the moment? Because I was being honest. I want him to fill me with our babies. Is that even possible before we bond and I gain some wolfiness?

"That right there, what is going on in your head, is the reason why we should have talked about it first." He tilts my chin up. "Every word that I said is true. I want babies with you. I want it all, right now. And if that is something that you want too then I say we go for it. But if it is too soon for you, I understand that too and we can keep drinking the tea until you are ready."

"I want babies with you too," I say after I let his words sink in. "Is it even possible for me to get pregnant before we bond?"

"I am not sure. Rowan and War got pregnant during their heat after the bonding. There are some non-shifter species in our world but the three of you are the only humans we know of."

"Well, we both drank the tea this morning anyway, so it won't make a difference this time. We are bonding in three weeks. Maybe we just wait until then?"

"We can do that." He takes my mouth in a lingering kiss.

"But in the meantime, can you still talk to me as if you are putting a baby in me? I think you unlocked a new kink."

"Is that so?" he growls as he tickles me.

"Mmhmm. I want to try everything. I want you to *teach* me everything."

"Fuck," he moans as he rocks his hard cock against me. "Teaching you might be a new kink for me."

"I can call you Professor next time, just to confirm of course," I offer.

The door to the library opens and Bade's father walks in. Bade turns quickly and blocks my body from view with his own as he lets out a loud growl.

"Mother help me!" his father exclaims as he averts his eyes. "Is no room safe anymore?"

"This one was supposed to be locked," Bade replies.

"Clearly it was not," Lycus mutters.

"Fucking War," Bade grumbles as he reaches for my dress and pulls it over my head.

Bade makes quick work of cleaning up the table while Lycus awkwardly steps over the books and papers on the ground on his way to finding the book that he came in for. I trail behind him and add the books back to the shelves, doing my best to not disintegrate due to embarrassment.

Feeling like I just got caught with my hand in the cookie jar, I give a brief apology to Lycus and practically run out of the room. Bade follows behind me laughing.

"That was so embarrassing!" I whisper-shout when he catches up to me. "What if he came in sooner?"

"Honestly, this happens to him more often than it should. He has nobody to blame but himself. If he would just take a moment to listen at the door before he barrels through it, it would save him from finding us in these situations. The first time he met Rowan, he walked right into War's room and found them together in bed."

"Like mid…"

"I think they had already finished."

"My ass was facing the door!"

"It is a very nice ass." I squeal as he reaches out to pinch me. "I promise it is going to be okay. We just need to think of a way to get back at War. He left that door unlocked on purpose. He might have even sent father to the library knowing that he would walk in on us."

"I'm sure Ro was in on it too. She likes to stir shit up when she is feeling anxious. Something about making the world outside reflect the chaos in her head is calming to her."

As we approach the door that leads to the garden, I reach out and grab Bade's arm. "War has a heightened sense of hearing, right?" Bade nods. "I have an idea of what we should do—but we should probably wait until they are settled with the babies. Maybe even offer to take them for the night."

"I'm listening…"

"Crickets."

Bade's booming laughter bounces off of the stone walls and follows us out into the garden where we join our little girl as she chases butterflies through the flowers.

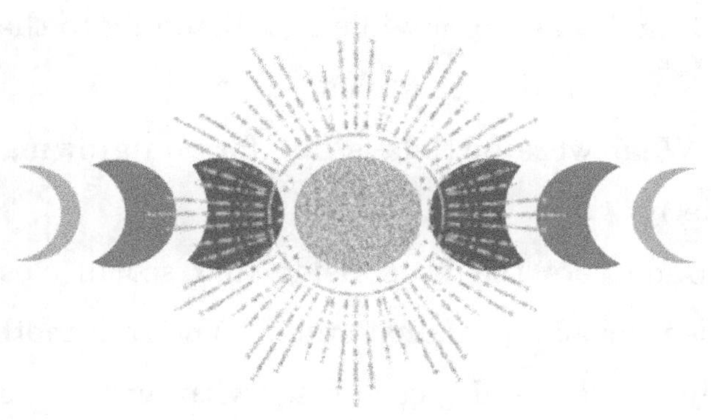

Chapter Twenty-One

It is nearing midnight and Bade and I are still awake. Curled up in my lap is a precious bear cub. Unsure as to when Juni will receive her Sun Kissed marking, we decided that it would be best for her to sleep with us tonight. I thought that Bade would need some convincing since we obviously would not be able to sleep like we have been lately—but he wanted to be here for Juni just as much as I do. There is just so much that we still don't know about this process, but we do know that it will only happen once in her life, and we do not want to miss it.

Will it hurt? Will it feel like the burning heat that I felt as the moon markings first showed on my skin?

Juni fell asleep a while ago, listening to the sound of Bade's voice as he read to us.

"What were birthdays like for you growing up?" I ask quietly.

Bade sets the book aside and scoots closer, his strong legs brushing against mine. "When our mother was still alive, we would celebrate with gifts and cake. Celebrating in the colder months usually meant small gatherings indoors–though we would also let our wolves run together as a family. We would stop at the hot springs and enjoy the heat before running back home for cake and games."

"That sounds really nice."

"It was," he agrees as he wraps his arm around my shoulders, careful to not jostle Juni too much. "After she died, our family did not celebrate much of anything. My brothers and I would still do the run, and Heka would make a cake for us to share, but it was never the same. Our uncle tried to get our father to spend the day with us, but he usually kept himself locked inside his room, tinkering with one of his many inventions. It was hard for him to be around us–to be around me. We all have her eyes, but I have her coloring. Our wolves looked so much alike, especially before I matured fully."

The pain in his voice makes my eyes well with tears. He has mentioned before that his father wasn't the same after his mother died, but I don't think I really understood how much it bled into every part of their lives. It is why he tried to push me away in the beginning. He doesn't want to lose himself if something happens to me. But I know, deep in my soul, that if anything ever did take me from this earth, Bade would still be there for Juni. She would be his reason to keep going. He would still celebrate birthdays. He would help teach her–help her grow up to be strong, caring, and kind. He would make sure that she felt loved every single day.

I turn his face to mine. "I love you," I tell him, brushing a kiss against his lips.

"I know," he replies with a smile. "I love you too. And I love our little girl." He gently places his hand on her back.

"I know," I echo with a matching smile.

He kisses my temple then asks, "What were birthdays like for you?"

I take my time to come up with the right words. Feeling brave enough to voice what I have never before said out loud, I say, "I don't even know for sure when my birthday is."

"What?" His look is so full of shock, but it also contains hints of anger. Not *at* me–but *for* me. He already knows that I was removed from my parents' care. But I haven't really told him just how little my parents were involved in my life.

"I was only two years old when we were taken from our parents and placed into foster care. They were not able to find any record of my birth. From what Ramsey was able to tell them, I was born at our home, and it was around Christmas–a holiday that is celebrated in the winter in our world. She was only six when I was born and was already the primary caregiver to Ro, who was two at the time. So, it was decided that my birthday was on Christmas Eve and the social worker filed whatever paperwork they needed to." I scoff. "I'm pretty sure that my parents did not even bother naming me. I think Ramsey did. We have a peanut butter and chocolate candy back in our world named Reese's Peanut Butter Cups. They have always been Ramsey's favorites. So, that's me. A girl without a birthday who was named after a candy bar."

"I'm so sorry, sweetheart."

"It is what it is." I shrug. "But, once we were in foster care, birthdays were celebrated in different ways. If I was placed with a family at the time, there was sometimes cake—maybe a gift. But usually, it just got lumped together with Christmas. If we were at a group home, the other kids would make cards. It was never really a big thing. The one thing that my sisters and I always did—whether we were together or not—is whisper a wish into our hands and then blow it out into the night, letting the wind carry it to the moon."

Realizing that I have tears falling down my cheeks, I quickly wipe them away.

"What did you wish for?"

"Sometimes a toy or a pretty dress." I chuckle. "Mostly, though, I wished for the moon to give us a family. A family that would want all three of us. Someone who could help take some of the weight from Ramsey's shoulders. Someone who could keep up with Rowan. Someone who could find me worthy of their love even though my parents didn't."

Bade kisses me deeply. He pours his love and his apology into the gentle strokes of his tongue.

Feeling Juni shift from her bear form, I pull my mouth away from Bade's and look down. Her entire body is lit up in a blinding gold. She shines so brightly, I have to squint my eyes. It is as if I was looking up at the sun. Bade and I sit in an awed silence. After a few minutes, the glow recedes, and her tan skin returns to its normal color. The only evidence of what just occurred is the metallic gold sunburst tattoo that rests on her right temple.

Rubbing her eyes, Juni sits up and looks around the room. "Is it mornin'?" she asks in a sleepy voice.

"Not yet, honey," I tell her. "But it is officially your birthday. You received your Sun Kissed mark."

Bade scoops her up out of the bed and carries her over to the mirror so that she can see. "How do you feel, Princess?"

"Okay. Just sleepy. It looks just like Nana's."

Bade carries her back over, snuggling her up against my front as he slides in behind me. I kiss her gently on her head, brushing her hair back from her face.

"Go back to sleep, Princess. We love you."

Juni yawns and shuts her eyes. Her little snores begin not long after.

Bade reaches across my body so that his arm is draped protectively over us both.

"Go to sleep, Wildflower. I love you," he whispers low in my ear.

"I love you too, Beast."

The next morning, I wake to the sounds of Juni giggling. I follow the sound and find Bade and Juni playing on the balcony. Bade is dressed up like a princess, complete with a crown and makeup, and they are having what looks to be a very fancy pretend tea party.

"Do you want a bit more sweets?" Juni asks in a silly voice.

"Any more and this tea will become candy," he replies.

"That's the only way it is yummy," she whispers as she adds a spoonful of sweetener into his cup.

I take a seat next to him before pulling Juni onto my lap.

"Happy Birthday, honey bear. I love you," I tell her with a squeeze.

"I love you too, Mommy." Her little voice saying those words soothes an ache in my soul that I didn't even realize was there. I look over to Bade and find his eyes glistening.

"Can I call you that? In my real dream my cousins call Auntie Ro 'Mommy' and Uncle War 'Daddy'. Can I use those words too?"

"We would love that very much, Princess," Bade replies since I am still lost in this feeling of rightness.

"When you have babies, will they call you Mommy and Daddy too?"

"Yes, sweetie. Those are words that children use in the world that I am from for their parents."

"I am yours even though I was already born when we met?"

"Yes. You are ours," Bade says. "And any babies that we might have in the future will be your brothers and sisters. It does not make any difference to us that you were already born when we all found each other. You are ours."

Juni reaches out and drags Bade into our hug. When she pulls away, she wipes tears off of both of our faces. "Are you sad?"

"No, honey. We are really happy," I tell her. "These are happy tears."

Juni smiles up at the sun. "I think Nana knew that I am yours," she says softly.

"Me too, honey."

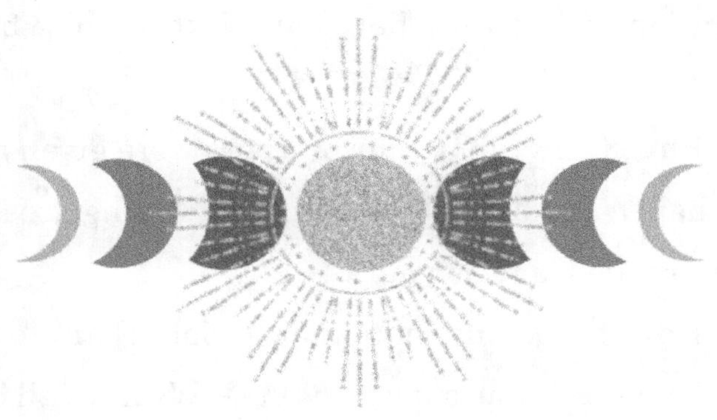

Chapter Twenty-Two

Bade

"I am not wearing this."

Reese snorts a laugh while we both get ready for our beach day. Rowan had the clothier design special clothes for us to wear in the water. A bathing suit. It is already ridiculous enough—the idea of not just swimming naked—but then to choose *this*?

"You are definitely wearing it," Reese says with a smile. "Besides, it matches mine and Juni's."

Matching in color—sure. The three of us were all given metallic gold bathing suits. They match Juni's sun kissed marking and the color looks amazing in combination with Reese's fiery hair. But that is where the similarities end.

"Plus, I saw what your brothers were given as well. Other than War's being blue and Griff's being green, they are exactly the same as yours."

"How is this any more appropriate than just being nude? I'm not even sure it will fit me." We have all become accustomed to the Hunt sisters' need for modesty. At least while we are out in public. But this…this just does not make sense.

"That is why you are trying it on now before you shift. Ro made sure that the clothier used material that is extra stretchy." She winks at me. I honestly cannot tell if she is serious about me wearing this or not. This must be a joke, right?

Apparently, it is not a joke. After running us through the forest, my brothers and I all drop our ladies off at the beach before going back into the trees to change. When Griff and I are both about to refuse to go through with this, War stops us in our tracks.

"You will do this," he demands. "If not because your Mates asked you to, then for me. Because *my* Mate is going to be in labor in a few hours and she has demanded that we wear these. So, chin up. Walk out there with pride that our Mates want to share things from their world with us. Move with confidence. We can do this. We *will* do this."

Griff and I both grunt in agreement and then the three of us emerge from the safety of the trees.

"Ow ow!" Rowan yells once she sees us. "Work it, Big Guy!"

Ramsey is folded in half, cackling at the sight. "Thank god I have a photographic memory. I want to remember this picture forever," she wheezes.

Reese and Juni are lost in a fit of laughter. "This is even sillier than my dream," Juni giggles.

"The speedos were definitely the way to go, Ro!" Reese shouts over the laughter. "Do you think they would pose for an artist?"

"For over the mantle?" Ramsey asks.

"Get Juni to ask," Rowan suggests. "She has them wrapped around her finger. Bat those eye lashes Princess!"

"That's it," I mumble as I take off in a run, scooping up my girls along the way, and diving into the lake as their squeals and laughter echo off of the water.

Once we break back through the surface, I hold Juni long enough to make sure that she can stay above the water before letting her go. Then, I pull Reese against me and squeeze her ass. Leaning in so only she will hear, I whisper, "We will cross spanking off of your list tonight."

"Don't threaten me with a good time, Beast," she whispers back before biting my ear.

Making sure to use Reese's body to help hide my inappropriately timed hard-on, we make our way over to the rest of our group and sit in the shallow water to watch Juni play. There are several other families here today, taking advantage of the water on this hot day. Juni soon joins a group of kids to play with, and we all enjoy a relaxing day in the water.

"Mommy!" Juni calls over to us a while later as she trudges through the knee-high water with a friend. "You are supposed to meet my new friend, Romy."

Reese extends her hand to greet the little girl. "It is nice to meet you, Romy."

When Romy hesitates to take Reese's hand, Juni says, "It's okay. You are supposed to shake it. Then just watch, okay?"

As soon as Romy touches Reese's hand, her moon markings and eyes light up silver. I move closer and put my hand on Reese's back just in case she falls.

"I told you," Juni whispers to her friend.

"Madoc, Nightfang, Madoc, Nightfang..." Reese repeats the same words over and over again until the glow recedes and she blinks and shakes her head.

"Madoc is Eden's son," Rowan says quietly.

"Are you from Nighthowl?" I guess. I know that she is not from Nightfury and if she was in Nightfang, she would have most likely already met Madoc.

Romy nods, still too shy to speak.

"Her parents are right here," Juni says as she points to a couple as they approach. Romy runs to her mother and clings to her legs.

"Hello," Reese greets. "I'm not sure if you know who I am..."

"You are the Nightfury Alpha's Mate," the mother says as they both bow their heads respectfully.

"Yes. And I have Moon Touched magic that allows me to have visions. I can help wolves find their True Mates. When I greeted your daughter, I had a vision of her Mate. He is a little boy in Nightfang."

Once the shock of what she told them sinks in, they pick their daughter up and hug her with tears in their eyes.

"We are True Mates as well. We always hoped that Romy would find hers one day," the father explains.

"Can we meet him?" the mother asks.

"Of course," I tell them.

"We can help set something up," Ramsey adds. "His mother recently gave birth to twins, but I know that they would love to meet you. Madoc's parents are True Mates as well."

"Thank you, Alphas," the mother says.

After the family leaves, Juni turns to keep playing as if what just happened is completely normal. And I guess, for her, it was.

"Are you okay?" I ask Reese. Her eyes are out of focus, and she rubs at her temples as if they are causing her pain.

"I think so. That one hurt my head for some reason."

Ramsey places her hand on Reese's head, using her powers to search for the cause of her headache.

"The nerve where your magic stems from is pulsing. It feels okay though. There isn't anything for me to fix," Ramsey says as she pulls her magic back into herself.

"Maybe because it was forced? Or because you aren't bonded yet?" Griff suggests.

I reposition us so that Reese can lean back on my chest and rest.

"We will figure it out," she yawns. "We are bonding soon, anyway. Right here, actually."

"Ooh, a beach wedding. Love it!" Ro says. "Maybe we should wear our matching swimsuits?"

Rowan, Ramsey, and Reese all laugh at the suggestion.

We stay at the lake, keeping cool while Juni plays with other kids in the sand and water. Reese has split her attention between Juni and her sisters, trying to help distract Rowan from her upcoming labor.

My attention has been focused on her. She is so fucking beautiful, my Wildflower. Her wild, fiery curls float around her in the wind and her golden bathing suit clings to her curves, leaving very little to the imagination. I can tell that her head is still bothering her. Ramsey tried again to help ease her headache, but she could not find anything to fix.

After a delicious dinner and cake, we help Juni get ready for bed and then walk Juni out to the balcony off her room.

"It is time to make your birthday wish. Have you ever made one before?" Reese asks Juni.

Juni shakes her head. I kneel beside them, not wanting to miss this moment.

"It's easy," Reese tells her. "Just hold your hands like a cup in front of your face. Then, quietly whisper your wish into your hands, hold it for a minute in your hands and your heart, and then blow it up to the moon."

Juni looks at Reese with pure wonder in her eyes. "And then it will come true?"

"Maybe not how you would expect, or right away, but mine came true," she tells her as she looks me in the eyes.

Her wish for a family.

I reach for her hand and place a gentle kiss on her palm.

"Will you make a wish with me?"

"Of course we will, honey," Reese replies.

"You will need to give her hand back to her, Daddy," Juni loudly whispers.

Reese snorts. "Busted."

I release Reese's hand with a wink and then hold my hands in front of my mouth like a cup. At the same time, we whisper our wishes into our hands, hold it there for a bit, and then blow our wishes up into the night sky.

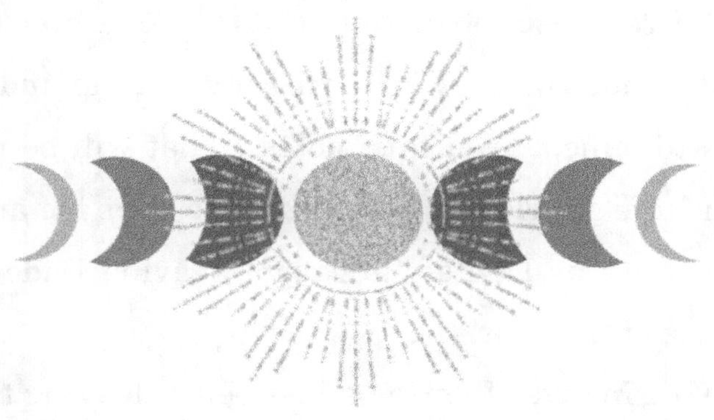

Chapter Twenty-Three

Bade and I make our way over to Ro and War's part of the house after we tuck Juni into bed. She was so tired after the day at the lake that she crashed before we even started reading her bedtime story.

"Are you ready for this?" I ask him as we get closer to their room.

He chuckles. "Am *I* ready? I am going to be spending the night hanging out with Griff. Are *you* ready?"

I chew on my bottom lip. "I don't do great with blood. I'm glad that I will only be there for moral support."

"If you need me or you need to take a break, I will be just outside the door." He tilts my chin up and brings his lips to mine. "And take notes. That will be us soon enough." He growls into my neck as he hugs me and then swats my ass as I enter Ro's room, leaving Bade on the other side of the door.

Griffin gives Ramsey a kiss before leaving through the door I just entered.

"Did your darling daughter happen to say what time I will be having these kids?" Ro's words are slightly gritted as she breathes through her contractions.

"Sometime tonight," I say as I cross the room to be by her side. "How are you doing so far?"

"Peachy," she grumbles. "Heka, do you have a cool cloth for War? He is looking pale."

"I do not like seeing you in pain," War replies. His face truly is an odd color. I can't tell if he is going to be sick or pass out.

"And I won't like seeing you pass out because you are so worried about me that you forget to breathe."

Ro begins pacing back and forth as she breathes through her contractions.

"Nobody is going to be passing out," Ramsey says. "War, walk with her, rub her back, make sure she doesn't topple over."

I help Heka prepare their bed while Ro is up and moving around. We remove all of their regular bedding and add layers of temporary blankets to protect the mattress.

It isn't long before we hear a splash against the stone flooring.

"Things are going to ramp up now," Ramsey whispers in my ear. I nod, thankful that she knows what she is doing.

Two hours later, Ro is giving birth to her third baby, a little girl, who is placed in my arms. Once the babies started coming, it all happened quickly. I have never seen anything so amazing as life being brought into the world.

Ro had a small tear, most likely caused by her second son who was born in his wolf form, but Ramsey was able to mend it immediately.

Both boys are blond while their little girl has a full head of black hair, just like Ramsey saw during her magical ultrasound.

After Ro is cleaned up and has held and fed all three babies, Bade and Griffin join us as we all marvel at their tiny, perfect faces. With each of the guys holding the newborns, Ro decides to share their names with us.

Pointing to Griffin, she says, "That little guy who was so eager to be born first is Archer. His brother," she points to Bade, "is Arrow. And this sweet little girl," she turns to War who is sitting next to her on the bed, "is Arden."

Nestling Archer, Arrow, and Arden into their cradles, we leave the new parents in the care of Heka and return to our room.

"I am so exhausted, and I hardly did anything," I confess, leaning up against Bade's arm as we walk through our room.

"It was a busy day. Good, though."

"It was amazing. I have never seen anything like that before. And, I was too busy giving War crap for almost passing out, that I completely forgot to pass out myself."

Bade chuckles at me. "Is that still something that you want? The experience did not scare you off?"

The flash of worry in his eyes makes mine soften towards him. "I have wanted a large family for as long as I can remember. Juni was an unexpected surprise—this entire world has been unexpected, actually. But I want this with you. I want it all. Every experience."

Bade backs me up until I am flush against the door. Grabbing the backs of my thighs, he lifts me, holding me in place with the press of his hips. A moan slips out of me as his hard body presses against my core.

"Are you too tired?" he asks me softly. And I know that he would stop. If I told him that I was too tired, he would kiss me silly and then lay me down in bed to rest. But I need him. I need him to fill me up and keep me full. My soul demands it.

I shake my head. "Please, Bade. Don't stop."

He growls into my neck as he works himself free from his pants. My clothes are torn from my body shortly after and he spears his cock into my already dripping pussy. We both moan as he seats himself fully, hiking my leg up to allow him in impossibly further.

"Tonight, we are going to practice." His words low, whispered into my ear. "I am going to fuck you hard against this door, but you need to be a good girl and keep those pretty little moans quiet. Can you do that for me?"

"Yes," I say against his neck as I scrape my teeth against his skin.

"Fuck," he groans as he unleashes himself on me. His thrusts are hard, steady, unrelenting—and I want them all. My orgasm builds so fast that I am not sure if he is there with me yet. So, I reach down and squeeze his knot. Hard. Just as I am tipped over the edge into bliss, I bite down hard on his shoulder to muffle my cries. I can feel his cum jetting into me as he takes my mouth with his and roars.

Still coming down from my release, I don't realize that we have made it to our bed until Bade pulls himself from me. I immediately whimper at the emptiness.

Bade chuckles as his head dips between my legs. "I am just going to heal you a bit and then you can have my cock back."

I start to tell him that I don't need any healing but then his tongue licks up my center and I am lost to the incredible feeling. I come twice more before he slides himself back into me, curling his body around mine and taking my mouth in a slow kiss.

"Go to sleep, Wildflower. I love you."

"I love you too," I mumble as I drift off into a deep sleep.

"Mommy! Daddy! Wake up!" I wake as a small body jumps on top of mine.

"What time is it?" My words are groggy, feeling like I haven't slept for more than a few hours.

"It is time for me to meet my cousins, silly." Juni's smile and excitement is infectious, bringing a smile to my face as well.

Before sitting up in bed, I look down and see that I am wearing one of Bade's shirts. He gives me a wink before crawling out of bed and heading for the bathroom. I pull Juni under the blankets with me and snuggle with her.

"I think that we should maybe give Ro and War some time to rest this morning before you meet the babies."

"I knew you would say that," she giggles. "I am just so excited!"

Bade comes back into our bedroom and jumps onto the bed with us. "I think we should go and have breakfast first. Then we can bring them some if they are up and ready for visitors. Does that sound like a plan?"

"I think they want waffles," Juni suggests with a sneaky smile.

"Do *they* want waffles, or do *you* want waffles?" Bade asks her.

"They do," she insists. "But…if we make some for them, can you make some for me too?"

After cleaning myself up for the day, I follow the sounds of laughter to find Bade and Juni covered in flour and Griffin and Ramsey bent over laughing.

"What happened?" I ask as I try to keep a straight face.

"I got a little messy and Daddy was jealous, so he got messy to match," Juni tells me as she mixes the ingredients in the bowl.

I look over to Bade, meeting his stare. There is something about my tough Viking being so gentle with our little girl that will make me melt every time. I walk over to him and seal my lips to his, forgetting for a moment that we are not the only ones in the room.

Ramsey clears her throat.

"Were you jealous too, Mommy? Now you match us."

I pull my mouth away from Bade's but wrap my arms tightly around his waist, pressing my face to his flour covered chest. "Yes, honey. I wanted to be just like you."

"You are like me, silly. We both have real dreams. And we both love Daddy."

"I need one," Griffin loudly whispers to Ramsey. She replies by smacking him gently on his stomach.

"I am going to take Juni to have a bath," Ramsey announces. "Sweets, you can finish making the breakfast while Bade and Reese help de-flour each other." She winks at me as she takes Juni's hand and leads her back to her room.

Turning in Bade's arms, I place a light kiss on his jaw. "You may have already deflowered me," I whisper, "but if you are a good boy and bathe quickly, there might still be time to *devour* me before breakfast is ready."

Griffin snorts from his spot over by the cooktop as Bade growls and tosses me over his shoulder.

And devour me, he did.

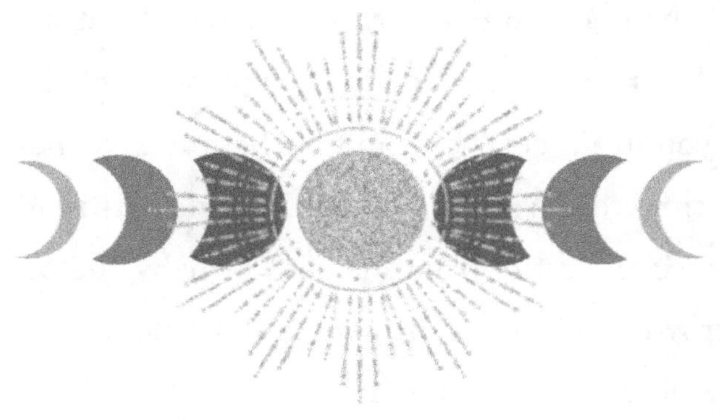

Chapter Twenty-Four

"What do you mean you lost him? How did he get away?" I growled at my Beta. After weeks of searching, Boone caught his brother's scent zigzagging over the border between Nightfury and the bears. He had been working with some bear shifter scouts and got lucky when Briggs got too close. The scent that he picked up led him to a remote cave system in bear territory where Briggs had most likely been hiding out this whole time. Aided by the scouts, they set up a perimeter while waiting for backup to arrive.

"There must have been a hidden tunnel. We had eyes on every known exit."

"And you are sure that those eyes can be trusted?"

"Yes. The bears do not want him anywhere near their territory. They have enough going on between rival clans to deal with a rogue wolf with a death sentence. Callum can be trusted. I have not scented deceit on him."

In addition to Boone being more levelheaded than his brother, he also has the ability to detect emotions and intentions by scent. It is a skill that we keep quiet for obvious reasons, but it has been useful in our military operations.

"We tried to smoke him out of the tunnels, but he did not resurface, nor was he found when we entered. He is a ghost once more."

"We need to find him. I do not trust that he will simply let this go."

"I agree. Callum has committed his clan to expanding and maintaining the perimeter around the cave system that he escaped into. We will do the same on our side. He cannot live underground forever."

"Find him."

I know that I should be there leading the team in finding Briggs. While Dreena's camp and most of her followers have been stomped out, there are still wolves that are loyal to their cause. We take more of her supporters into custody every day, spreading them between my outposts so that they are not able to organize themselves again. After Briggs is found, we will figure out what is to be done with the surviving supporters. Hopefully, without a leader, they will realize that their beliefs are based on lies and they will fall back into line. If not, they will be exiled or executed–depending on if they remain peaceful or resort to violence.

Even knowing that I should be out there leading the team, I cannot. My wolf will not allow me to be away from Reese or Juni while the threat to my Mate and her sisters is still out there. They would be safe at one of my outposts, but traveling there would pose some risks. And, Reese has not felt well enough to even leave the lodge for the last several days. Between her cycle and her visions, she has been laid up in bed with headaches. Ramsey has not been able to heal her, and we are hopeful that our bonding ceremony in a couple of days will help.

"What has you extra growly today?" War asks, jarring me from my thoughts. He has dark circles under his eyes and smells like spit up. Fatherhood is definitely a different look for him.

"Boone just let me know that Briggs slipped away from them again."

"How did that happen?" That is the question, isn't it?

"He is using some underground cave system. They have all of the known exits under guard with the help of the bears but he must have found another way out. I fucking hate that he is still out there posing a threat."

War grumbles in agreement. "How is Reese feeling? Any better?"

"She has been awake more today, but her body is weak. I was just on my way to find her some food. How are you doing? Are the pups still up all night?"

"One of them is always up and hungry. It is a constant rotation throughout the night. I feel like I spend most of the night swapping babies for Ro so that she can get some sleep while nursing them. I do not know how she does it. Last night, she told me that she wishes she had more nipples so that they could just stay latched on all night and I seriously considered asking Ramsey if she had the power to make that happen for her."

I chuckle.

"Just wait," he laughs. "I have a feeling that you will be joining the club sooner rather than later."

"I do already have a child, you know."

"Oh, I know. You have a beautiful daughter who sleeps through the night in her own room and only occasionally interrupts alone time with your Mate."

"Once they do not need to nurse all night, we will take some overnights so that you can sneak away with Ro. I am sure that Griff and Ramsey will help out too."

"Fuck," War curses, "The meeting between Romy and Madoc and their families is starting in a few minutes. I was supposed to be there to help make introductions. Do you think I can go like this?"

I look him over, unsure as to how honest to be. He must see the hesitation on my face because he looks down to notice the stains on his pants. "They are parents too. I am sure that they will understand," I assure him. "I thought that Griff and Ramsey were setting up this meeting." We walk together towards the front door. The meeting was planned to take place in one of our private meeting rooms off of the entryway.

"They got called out to a delivery. Griff was going to reschedule but Eden and Arlo are supposed to move to fill the position at the outpost that Sylas vacated. We need to figure out how to make it all work with Romy's family."

"Should they even be having this meeting? If the pups have not met yet, their pull should not be strong at this age."

"They ran into each other at the market the other day. Now Madoc has been sleepwalking, trying to find Romy again."

"And they cannot just stay?" I know War has not forgiven Eden for her betrayal, but the main village is large enough that he wouldn't need to ever see her if he didn't want to.

"They can. But Arlo and Eden want to go. They never stay in the big village for longer than they need to. Now that their babies are old enough to travel, they are itching to leave. And things have not been the same for them around here ever since Eden led Ro into that trap. Ro may have forgiven her, but the Pack has not forgotten."

War opens the door, and two wolf pups come barreling in, play-fighting and tackling each other. They are followed by their parents.

"Would you like me to take the pups back to the garden to play with Juni?" Both sets of parents give me nods so I reach down and scoop both pups up. "Come on, rascals."

I do not envy my brothers. While there are families in my pack, most know that they will be stationed in the big village after they have pups. Other than Tempest and Wrath, outposts in Nightfury are pretty remote and are not set up to support family life. Now that I have a family that will travel with me, I might need to make some changes.

"Juni," I call out to her from across the garden. "I have a couple of pups who would like to play." She smiles when she sees Madoc and Romy in their wolf forms and changes into a bear cub as she runs over. Her brown coat, which matches her hair, is now marked with a light golden sunburst near her right eye. I drop down to my knees as she gets close, chuckling as she tackles me to the ground. "Love you, Princess," I tell her as I scratch behind her ears. "Have fun with your friends." She nuzzles her head against my hand and then takes off after the pups. I wave to my father and Sylas before I head back to the kitchen to find some food for Reese.

When I walk into the kitchen, I find Reese and Rowan sharing a pan of cobbler while juggling the babies. I give Reese a kiss and then take all three of the babies from their arms and hold them against my chest while they sleep.

"How are you feeling?" I keep my voice quiet, not wanting to wake them.

"A lot better," Reese replies as Rowan says, "Tired."

"I think the worst of it is over," Reese adds.

"Are you sure that you will feel well enough for the ceremony?"

"And after the ceremony," Rowan mumbles around her fork.

"Ro!" Reese scolds as her cheeks turn my favorite shade of pink. She looks up at me through her lashes. "Nothing will keep me from bonding with you." A low growl rumbles from my chest, my wolf loving the eagerness of our Mate.

"Shhh!" Rowan whispers. "No waking the babies. This is the first time they have all slept at the same time. Ever. I'm not sure if I should eat, sleep, or bathe."

"Why not try to do all three? Bade and I can handle them for a bit."

"Seriously?" She asks. When we both nod, she grabs a sandwich and practically runs out the door as she whisper-shouts, "I'm not going to turn that offer down. Just bring them to me if they get hungry! Thanks!"

Making sure that Reese grabs a sandwich for herself, we make our way to some comfortable seating. I cannot help but notice a flash of heat in her eyes as I fold myself into a chair, keeping as steady as possible so that I do not wake the babies.

"What is that look for?" I ask quietly, with a smirk.

Her cheeks blush further. "I just forget that this is real sometimes. You have lived in my dreams for as long as I can remember. I catch myself wishing to never wake up. And then you have to go all daddy Viking and make me horny."

"This is doing it for you, huh?" I gesture towards the babies drooling on my chest.

She sighs. "It really is." I chuckle quietly. Hopefully she will still feel this way when I am exhausted and covered in spit up like War.

We sit in comfortable silence for a while, just soaking up the quiet before the lodge will inevitably return to chaos.

"Ramsey has set up a room in their wing for Juni. That way, our quarters will be completely private after our bonding," Reese says as she breaks the silence.

"That is a good idea. I have not been around during a heat before but if it is anything like what my brothers have told me, we are not going to want any interruptions."

Now that there will be so many children in the lodge, maybe it is time that we expand. We could add a wing just for the children so that they do not need to switch rooms every time a heat hits. The lodge has always belonged to the Night family, but it was never meant to house three Alphas and their families. Until us, there only ever was one Alpha. Sometimes the Beta would also live at the lodge, with a family if they had one. Staff and guests have always stayed in the cabins on our property. I know that Griff and War are both busy right now, so I make a mental note to run the idea past them. It would not surprise me if it is something that Griff has already started planning.

"Do you have any questions about the ceremony? Or, after?" I ask knowing that she has talked to her sisters about it, but I want to make sure that she is going to be comfortable.

"My sisters told me about their ceremonies, and I did get a sneak peek during that vision a few weeks ago. It is basically like a wedding, right? But with more biting and less clothes?"

I chuckle at the simplification. "In addition to magically tying our bodies and souls together, transferring powers, and making me the luckiest wolf in the world, that is the general idea, yes."

"And we *need* to be naked? Isn't that going to be weird? Your dad and grandmother are going to be there."

I pull her onto my lap, adjusting the babies so that there is room for her. I bring her hand up to my mouth and give her a gentle kiss. "I know that nudity is not as socially accepted in the world that you came from, but here, it is not something that is really even thought about. Some shifters choose to wear clothing to help stay warm in the colder seasons. Some do not. Others might choose to wear clothing because they like the way that it looks."

"My memories of when I was captured are not clear, but I do remember that, I guess."

"Before Rowan arrived here, Griff was the only one of us who wore pants consistently."

Reese snorts. "I do prefer you without clothes. But bare asses on the couch? Seriously? I am never going to look at family dinner or game night the same again."

"Well don't you look cozy?" War asks as he enters the room with Juni on his shoulders. "Practicing for about six months from now?"

"Uncle War! Are you talkin' bout my sisters?" Reese locks eyes with mine, her smile matching my own. "I thought that was a real dream that was supposed to stay in my head. Should I have told you?" Juni worries her bottom lip, just like Reese does when she is trying to figure something out.

War mouths "sorry" and takes his pups from me so that Juni can crawl into my lap next to Reese.

"Juni, you can always tell us about your visions," I reassure her.

"We will work together to learn which real dreams we keep to ourselves and which ones we share with others. But Daddy is right, honey bear, you can always tell us. Okay?"

"Okay," she agrees with a smile.

"For this particular real dream," Reese continues, "let's keep any other details in your head for right now. Is that okay?"

"Yep!" She snuggles into my chest, trying her best to wrap her little arms around both of us.

"We love you so much, Princess."

The three of us stayed like that for a while. Our little family, pulled together by fate.

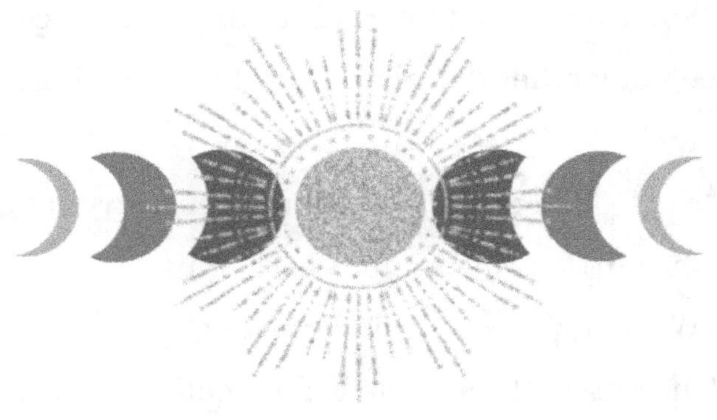

Chapter Twenty-Five

Reese

I awake mid-moan; a cool summer breeze brushes against my bare ass as it is lifted further into the air. Bade has me positioned on my knees, with a pillow wedged under me for support as he nips at my thighs and plunges his thick fingers in and out of me.

"Fuck, Wildflower. You must have been having a great dream. Your pussy was squeezing me so tight, I had to get a taste."

I moan again as he does just that. Licking straight through my center, he swirls his tongue around my ass before returning to flick my clit.

"Tell me about your dream, sweetheart. Maybe I can make it happen right now."

I feel my cheeks heat, nervous to share but wanting it to happen so badly. His fingers slow and he pulls his face away, waiting for me to answer.

"My hands were tied, and I had a blindfold on." I tell him breathlessly.

Bade's body pulls away from mine and I whimper at the loss of his heat. I watch as he disappears into the bathroom, returning with a length of soft leather and what looks to be a torn piece of a shirt. Keeping me positioned with my ass in the air, he binds my wrists behind my back with the leather and uses the fabric as a blindfold. "If you want to stop at any point, just say stop," he whispers in my ear. "What else happened in your dream?"

Everything is more intense this way. He lightly trails his hand down my spine, working his way down to my dripping core. He teases me, not quite touching where I need him most. "What happened in your dream, Wildflower?"

I am panting, already so needy for him. "You filled me up. With your cock and your fingers. At the same time."

"Hard?" He spanks my pussy, the little bit of pain making me gush down my thighs. "Or gentle?" He leans in and laps at the mess he just made.

"Ha...hard," I moan as he does not let up. "And then gentle."

"Good girl," he growls into my ear as he collects my wetness with his fingers, following my slit up to my back hole. I hear him spit and feel as it drips down my crack.

"Please," I whimper.

Bade groans as he lines his head up with my entrance and slowly pushes inside, his finger doing the same to my ass.

"Breathe, sweetheart." I hadn't realized that I stopped. Once his knot is pressing against my pussy, he pauses to allow my body to adjust. I take a deep breath, and he starts to move. The first couple of thrusts are gentle, testing to make sure that I am wet enough for what he is about to give me. What I need.

And then, he unleashes himself on me. His thrusts set a punishing rhythm, hitting hard and deep in a spot that only he could reach. With my hands tied and my sight blocked, my other senses are heightened. Everything is more intense. I am overwhelmed by the sounds and smells of sex, the feel of his body filling mine to bursting. My orgasm crashes over me so quickly, I am unable to muffle my cries. Bade bites down on the back of my neck, careful not to break the skin, as he loses himself inside me.

I am still lost in the endless waves of my release when Bade pulls himself free from my body, flipping me over onto my back. His lips kiss and nibble all over my neck, breasts, and hips before he latches his mouth over my sensitive clit and sucks. Hard. I cry out, squeezing his head with my thighs. I can hear a low laugh before his tongue soothes my bruised pussy. He works his finger back into my ass, adding a second one to stretch me as his tongue teases and fucks my fluttering walls, making me come again.

His mouth comes up to meet mine as he unties my blindfold and wrist bindings, rubbing my wrists to make sure that they are unharmed. He leaves me in the middle of the bed, stars still sparking in my eyes as I stare blissfully at the ceiling. Returning with a warm cloth, he cleans me up before crawling back into bed with me, tucking me close into his side. I roll on top of him, impaling myself back onto his stiff cock. Humming in pleasure as I lower my head to his chest.

"Go to sleep, love. I will be here when you wake." Listening to the sound of his heart, knowing that it beats in time with my own, I relax into a deep, dreamless sleep.

Waking slowly the next morning to sounds of others moving around in the hall, I keep my eyes closed and soak in this blissful morning just a little longer. It is rare for Bade to still be sleeping when I wake up in the morning. His arms wrapped around me. His cock still inside me. I give him a little squeeze, pulling a low moan from his sleepy lips.

"I told you she didn't need the 'what to expect on your wedding night' sex talk." I shriek as Ro's voice jars both of us from our blissed-out stupors.

Bade covers my body with his, growling towards the door until he realizes that it is just my nosy sisters who have invaded our space.

"Yes, yes. You are really scary. Please don't crush our sister," Ro says dryly.

"Did you think that maybe you should knock?" I ask them as I try to wiggle free from Bade. His body relaxes a bit, but he does not let me go, burying his face into my neck and grumbling about wanting to go back to sleep.

"We did," Ramsey says. "And you guys missed breakfast. Trouble sleeping?"

Bade sneakily licks my neck, reigniting heat from last night. I squeal as he laughs, finally releasing me as he slides out of bed and walks to the bathroom. Ramsey respectfully looks up at the ceiling while Rowan makes no effort to look away from my Mate's perfect ass. I throw a pillow at her face.

He returns shortly after, now wearing a pair of pants, and tosses me his shirt. "I am going to find you some breakfast."

"Is a little privacy too much to ask for?" I ask my sisters as I pull the shirt on before climbing out of bed.

"We have shared bath water. It isn't anything we haven't seen before." Ro has a point.

"And the reason for this in person wakeup call?" I ask as they follow me into the bathroom, not a care in the world as I walk over to the toilet to pee.

"A wellness check. I was up feeding the babies early this morning and thought I heard a scream. When you didn't show yourself at breakfast, we felt it necessary to make sure that you were not murdered. You're welcome."

"Oh my god!" Heat burns my cheeks as I remember exactly what caused that scream last night.

"Clearly she was being taken care of, not murdered." Ramsey has the decency to try and hide her laugh.

"For real though, we just wanted to hang out with you today since your bonding is tonight."

"Before my ceremony, Heka lathered me in oils, gave me an awkward sex talk—with diagrams, and then I freaked out about having to walk naked through a pack of people that I did not know well."

"Now that you know that I do not need the sex talk, you are here to lather me in oils?"

She snorts. "You know I would. But I mostly wanted to make sure that you are not freaking out."

"I'm not. Instead of picturing everyone in the audience naked, I am just going to pretend like I am wearing clothes."

"We have Juni all set up in our wing. Lycus and Sylas are set to step in if we are called away for a delivery. And, I brought a bag of tea over so that you guys have some on hand for during the heat."

"We actually won't need any," I quietly admit.

Ramsey's eyes go wide, clearly shocked by my confession. "Are you..."

"Not yet. Though, a little bear may have let it slip that I will be soon."

Ro squeals and pulls me into a hug. Ramsey's reaction is calmer, though her eyes turn a little misty. By the time Bade returns with food, he finds us all crying in the bathroom.

"What happened?" He crosses the room and lifts my face to wipe my tears. He must have alerted his brothers to our distress because they came barging into the room, babies in their arms and Juni at their heels.

"Happy tears," I assure him. "We are just really happy." My sisters nod in agreement, putting their Mates at ease. Looking around the bathroom, packed full of my family, I can't help but allow more happy tears to fall.

This, right here, is my moon wish come true.

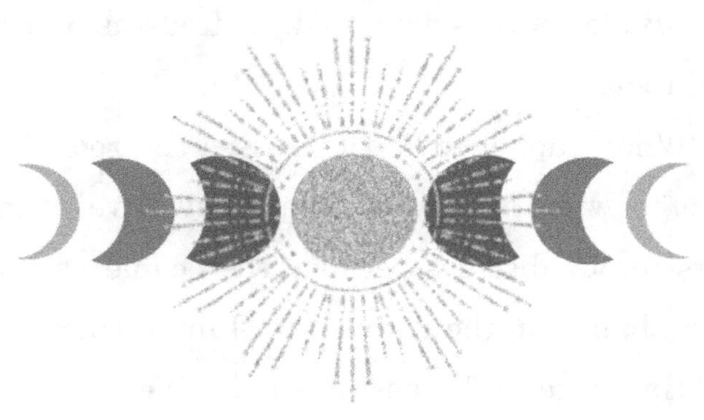

Chapter Twenty-Six

I spent the entire day being pampered with my sisters, Juni, and the babies. The guys insisted that we lock ourselves in the Nighthowl wing, using their massive bathroom which had been set up like a spa. They even brought in staff so that we could receive massages, manicures, and pedicures. I am so relaxed, I feel a little tipsy.

"Are you having fun, honey?" Juni has loved the princess treatment we have all been receiving today.

"Yes! I can't wait to show Daddy my fingers and toes. Do you think he will want pink paint to match us?"

Chuckling, I give her a squeeze. "I think you could talk him into it. He would do anything for you, you know."

"For us," she corrects. Bopping me on the nose.

"For us."

I help her into her dress made entirely from flowers. I have no idea how they were able to make it, but when I described my vision to my sisters, they talked to the clothier and brought it to life. Literally, in Ro's case. She grew all of the flowers for the ceremony, including the flower crown that adorns my head. Colorful wildflowers, just like Bade's name for me.

"Do you know what you are going to say during the ceremony?" Ramsey gently pins my hair back, taming the wild mess of curls just enough so that none fall in my face.

"Not a clue. I'm hoping that the words will find me when it is time."

"Just speak from the heart." She squeezes my shoulder, spinning me around to face her. "I can't believe that my baby is getting married."

I lean in and give her a tight hug. "Thank you for always taking care of me—of us." Ro walks over to join our hug. "I am so happy that you are here with me today."

"It's time," Ramsey whispers. I look out the window, noticing that the sun has dipped low, painting the summer sky in rose gold and violet. I take Juni's hand while my sisters hold Arden, Arrow, and Archer. The lake is a little ways away from the lodge so we will be arriving by sleds, pulled by Nightfury wolves. My polished skin is wrapped in a silky robe, giving me a few more minutes of privacy before I bare it all under the moon.

Once we arrive, my sisters make their way to their Mates, leaving Juni and I alone to walk down the aisle. Taking a deep breath, I slip out of my robe, leaving me in only the beautiful, jeweled ceremonial cuffs and flower crown. My long hair covers my chest and the light from the now risen moon reflects off of my skin like stardust.

Juni and I make our way towards the flowered arch on the beach of the lake. Bade stands tall with so much love in his eyes that it almost hurts. My heart attempts to burst from my chest. He leaves his spot under the arch and meets us part way down the aisle. Crouching down to his knees, he holds out a small pouch. Spilling the contents into his hand, he reaches for Juni's and my clasped hands. Unsure as to what is happening, I follow his lead and kneel down with him.

"It was explained to me that in the world that you came from, it is customary to give jewelry as a way to show our love and commitment to each other. So, I had these made. I wanted both of you to have these tangible reminders of my commitment to you and our family."

He raises Juni's arm and clasps a golden bracelet onto her wrist. The chain is adorned with a cluster of tiny bright jewels. "Becoming your Daddy has been one of the greatest joys in my life. I want you to know that fate may have brought us together, but we choose you to be ours. Every day and always."

"I love you," Juni says as she wraps her little arms around both of us.

"We love you too, Princess," I tell her as I hold onto her just a little longer.

Finally breaking away, Ramsey meets us at the aisle and takes Juni's little hand in her own, leading her over to where she can watch the rest of the ceremony.

Bade and I finish the walk to the beach, standing in front of the flowered arch. While I know that there are several people here watching us, it feels as if we are the only two people in the entire world.

I gasp as Bade takes my hand and slips a beautiful ring onto my finger. It is the perfect match to Juni's bracelet. The golden band is decorated with clusters of tiny, colorful gems. Like a field of Wildflowers on a sunny day.

"Do you know why I call you Wildflower?" Bade's voice is gentle, his eyes turning a deep blue that only happens when he looks at me.

I shake my head, realizing that I have never once asked where that nickname came from.

"Flowers are seemingly fragile, delicate. Most would assume that they are easily crushed, trampled, damaged. While that is true for some, it is not true for all. Wildflowers are built to withstand harsh weather. They are the first to rise up after a drought or a fire. They take whatever has been thrown at them and add their own beauty. Their own strength. They make The Mother come back to life when it seems like there is nothing left. You are my Wildflower." I gasp at his words as his hand comes up to cradle my cheek. "You always have been—even when I was afraid to let you in. You withstood the harsh circumstances that you were forced into when you first arrived here. You fought my fire with your inner strength. You found cracks in my foundation, planting your roots and rising up towards the sun. You added beauty and hope and love into my world. Our world. That is why you are my Wildflower. And I am so fucking in love with you."

It is all too much. Not only the thoughtfulness that was put into the ring that he gave me, but to also have a piece made for Juni. The daughter that he welcomed without hesitation as soon as he learned about her. He never once questioned her role in our lives. Hearing the way that he sees me. Truly sees me—in a way that nobody has ever done before. I have always been the "sweet" one. The "soft, delicate" one. Never have I been the strong one. I rise up on my toes to offer my lips to him. My Mate. The one my soul calls out to.

Pulling away breathless, I let my words flow out from my heart. "All I have ever wanted was a family. My childhood was spent bouncing between homes, staying only long enough to begin feeling comfortable before starting fresh again. Never really finding my place in the world. Before finding you, my entire life was centered around the need to survive, not thrive. That was all I was ever doing. But each year on my birthday, I allowed myself one wish. I let myself hope for the life that I wanted to live. A life that included a family that would accept me and my sisters. A family that would support, encourage, and love us in a way that we have never experienced before. A family that gives all of us the opportunity to thrive. You are the man of my dreams—not only because you visited me in my dreams long before I met you, but also because you allow me to do just that. Dream. With you, I know that I am safe to want. I am safe to dream. Safe to love, hope, and care."

"You are always safe with me," he says, eyes glassy.

"I know. And now I know why I was never able to find a home. My place was never in that world. It was always here, with the other part of my soul—with you. Fate may have helped bring us together but even without that, I would still choose you. I choose this life that we are building together. A life where you not only follow me into my dreams but also stand beside me in the light."

"I choose you, too." Bade crashes his mouth to mine, stealing my breath as he reinforces his words. "Are you ready?"

I nod, feeling nervous but never so certain in my entire life. We both search for Juni one last time, knowing that it will be several days before we see her again. Ramsey teaches her to blow us a kiss, which we return before turning back to each other.

"You are mine," he whispers before bringing his mouth to my neck, piercing my skin, and taking a deep pull of my blood. My entire body heats, causing a bottomless ache to settle in my core.

"You are mine," I repeat before biting down on his neck until the coppery taste of his blood floods my mouth. He groans against my neck as he gently laps at the puncture marks that he left on my skin.

I am vaguely aware of cheers coming from our family and friends, already fighting the early haze of heat. Bade's tongue licks up my neck before he takes my mouth with his own. I whimper, squeezing my legs together. "I need you," I say quietly against his lips.

Without warning, Bade shifts, his huge golden colored wolf scooping me onto his back as he makes a break for home. Once we are far enough away from the crowd, I allow a moan to escape.

"Take your hand and rub that perfectly needy pussy, Wildflower." Bade growls the words directly into my mind. I knew that we would be able to communicate like this after our bond, but I didn't realize how amazing it would feel to share this connection with him. To have him literally in my head, able to communicate even when it is impossible for words to leave my lips.

Holding on to his fur with one hand, I lower the other between my legs, rubbing circles over my clit. *"I need more,"* I whine.

"Add your fingers, start with three. You are dripping down my back, sweetheart."

I spear three fingers into my center as I grind myself down against his back. It is just enough to push me over the edge. I nearly fall from his back as my body convulses in pleasure. I am still feeling the after waves of my orgasm as we burst through the doors of the lodge. Bade shifts as we approach our wing, catching me with his arms and pressing me against the door to our suite, locking the rest of the world out with a quick flick of his hand.

Bringing my hand to his mouth, he sucks my release from my fingers and slams his cock up into me. "Fuck, Reese," he groans. "I cannot be gentle with you right now."

"I don't need gentle. I need you to fuck me. Claim me. Fill me to bursting."

"Fuck!" The door behind me rattles as his cock thrusts into me at a relentless pace. His large hands grip my ass, his finger teasing my hole with the promise of more. I moan as he hits that perfect spot inside me over and over.

"I'm so close, baby. I want your knot. I need it."

Bade lowers his head, pulling my breast into his mouth, sucking so hard that I feel it in my clit. He spins us around, walking me over to our bed and lowering me down onto my back. His thrusts become harder, more intense, as he works his knot into my pulsing heat. Bade roars as my walls clamp around his knot, locking us together for the first time and forever.

Tears stream down my face as the most intense orgasm I have ever had rockets my body into another dimension. Our entire existence shattered and remade as we float, just the two of us, in a night sky full of stars. The feeling of his essence pouring into me and the sounds of our ragged breathing, the only ties to reality.

"Are you okay?" Blinking the stars from my eyes, I look up to find my Mate with a flash of worry on his face.

"That was perfect," I reply, not realizing that I said it with my mind until he huffs a laugh, adjusting us so that I am not crushed under the weight of his muscles.

Bade gently wipes the tears from my cheeks before lifting my chin and drawing me into a lazy kiss. Needing more, I push the kiss deeper, pulling his tongue into my mouth as I roll to straddle his hips. We are still knotted together so I gently roll my hips, grinding my clit against his pelvic bone.

He groans. "You are so fucking beautiful, Reese."

"So are you." I touch my fingers to his temple, tracing the lines of his moon markings and then further down, touching his lips, chin, neck, pressing lightly on the bite that I left earlier. Bade moans loudly, thrusting his hips. Leaning down, I suck on that sensitive mark, bruising the skin and reopening the bite. The taste of his blood resettles my soul. Bade curses and ruts into me, spilling his seed deep inside me over and over again.

Smiling, I lay my head down on his chest and fall asleep.

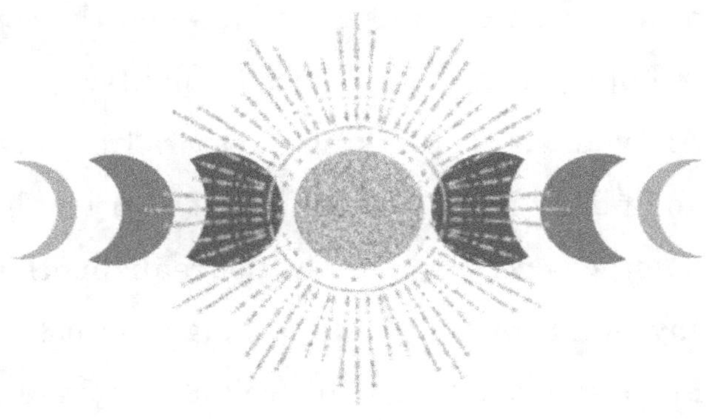

Chapter Twenty-Seven

"You look so pretty choking on my cock," I tell Reese as she moans, sending a vibration straight to my balls. We have been fucking for four days straight, only pausing long enough to hydrate or rest when our bodies force us to.

I woke up a few minutes ago to my Mate lowering her mouth over my cock, unable to take all of me but so damn determined to try.

"Bring that pretty pussy over here so I can get a taste."

She flips her body around, positioning her knees on each side of my head, giving me the best fucking view I have ever seen. "Sit on my face, Wildflower. Do not be shy. Grind that pussy on me."

She moans at my words, and I watch as our mixed arousal gushes down her thighs, dripping onto my face. Reaching my hands up, I use one to pull her down to my mouth. The other joins my cock in her mouth, gathering a mixture of her spit and the cum that is weeping out of my cock. Once it is nice and wet, I push my finger into her asshole, stretching her while I feast on her pussy.

"I am going to spill down your throat. Swallow it all like the good girl that you are." I spear my tongue and finger into her in time with the delicious rhythm she has set with her mouth. Adding another finger into her ass, she moans and spasms finding her release and drowning me in her cum. She milks my fingers just like she is sucking my cock and squeezes my knot with her hand. My seed coats her throat. She does not waste a drop.

Reese whimpers at the loss of my fingers as I reposition us. I pull her up to my mouth, kissing her deeply before rolling her onto her stomach and plunging my still hard cock into her soaked channel, getting it nice and wet. Pulling out, I press the head of my cock against her asshole. "I have filled your pussy and your mouth, are you ready for me to claim this virgin hole?" I apply light pressure, not actually entering her but teasing her while she decides.

"I don't think you will fit," she pants out.

"We will make it fit." I press in just a bit. "Your greedy ass is already trying to suck me in. Please tell me I can fuck you here."

She nods her head, her face pressed against the bed.

"I need your words before I do this, sweetheart."

"Please fuck my ass, Beast. I need to feel you everywhere."

A low growl rumbles from my chest, pleased that she is allowing–wanting–this to happen. I have fucked plenty of asses in my many years–females, males, it was never anything more than a tight hole for me to find a release in. But everything is different with Reese. Wanting to make sure that I do not hurt her, I go slow, pressing in at a steady rate, allowing her to adjust to my size as I fill her. "Breathe, love. You are taking me so well." I reach around to rub her clit, relaxing her further so that I can keep working myself into her.

"So. Full."

"So tight." I grit my teeth, putting most of my energy into holding myself back. I do not look down until I feel my balls hit my hand that is on her clit. "Push yourself back towards me. Such a good girl." She is squeezing me so tight, I am about to embarrass myself with how quickly this is going to happen. When I feel her back into me, I know she is ready for me to move. Pulling out until only my head remains, I thrust back in, one smooth, firm motion. Her moans are low, coming from a place deep inside her. Pulling her up so that her back is flush against my chest, I take her mouth with mine. I continue fucking in and out of her until she is screaming my name and clamping around my cock so hard that I cannot pull out. I flood her ass with so much cum that it is leaking out all over our thighs.

Gently, I pull myself out of her and lay us down on our sides. My wolf reminds me that I need to get us into a bath, clean up the bed, get her to eat and drink something. But right now, all I can do is hold her.

"I didn't know it could be like this," she mumbles, already falling asleep.

"Me either," I confess. It has never been like this before.

"I think the heat is ending." Sadness takes over her expression as she turns and buries her face against my neck. I can feel her tears as she presses herself closer.

"Hey, it is okay," I tell her as I rub her back. "Talk to me, sweetheart."

"I'm just going to miss this. I'm not sure I am ready to go back to being a regular person again."

"This was not a one-time thing, you know. The bonding, sure, but heats will happen again. And in the meantime, I plan on knotting you every chance we get. We do not need to rush back into reality. We can take the rest of today and tonight, see how we feel in the morning. Okay?"

"Okay," she says quietly. "We should probably get cleaned up." Reese looks around the room, noticing the pile of dirty bedding and plates and cups littering the space, and wrinkles her nose. "This whole room will need to be deep cleaned. I don't even remember us being over there!" I snort as she points out the desk that had been swiped clear of its papers and now sits at an angle.

"You are doing great things for my ego."

Reese giggles. "I remember your giant cock. The locations that we banged in are just a little hazy."

My laugh is loud and deep. "Well as long as you remember my giant cock."

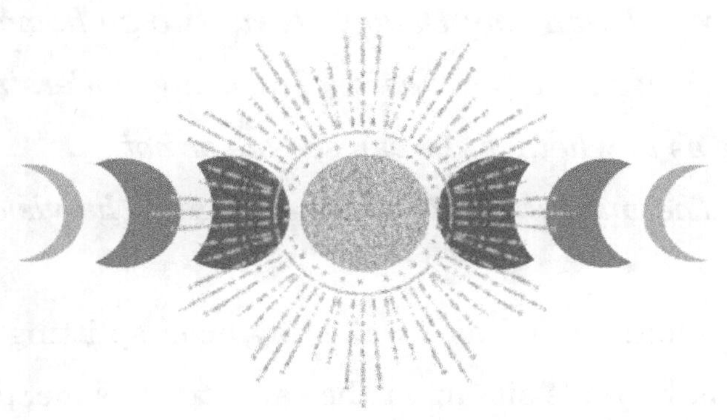

Chapter Twenty-Eight

"I don't like it here. It's too dark." Juni's lip trembles as she folds herself up tight. I look around, noticing the walls made of stone and packed dirt. She is in a tunnel or a cave. "I want my Mommy and Daddy."

"Shut up, brat. It is their fault that you are here." The voice is gruff. It feels familiar but I don't know where I have heard it before.

I try to call out to her, but she can't hear me. It is as if I am just peeking in, watching a movie as it plays out in front of me.

"I am thirsty. It is too warm. The water is stinky." She is looking directly at me as she speaks. It is a

 "I want my Daddy. I want to go home." *She rubs her fist over her heart. I nod my understanding, unsure as to whether she can see me or not.*

The man stalks towards Juni and the vision cuts out.

"Juni!" I yell as I wake, my head splitting with a sharp pain. Bade sits up at the same time as me, panting and holding his head. "Did you see it too?"

"Yes. What was that?" We both hurry to climb out of bed, racing to the door. Naked, we race through the lodge in search of our little girl. Finding the room that she was staying in empty, we burst into Ramsey and Griffin's room, finding them both asleep.

"Where is she?" Bade roars, searching in every room of their suite.

"What's happening? What is wrong?" Ramsey asks, frantically looking around trying to figure out why we just barged into her room before dawn.

"She is gone. Juni is gone." The words come out of my mouth as sobs. How did this happen?

"Briggs took her," Bade growls.

"Is that who that man was? I couldn't see his face." Bade nods, his hands shaking at his side.

"That is not possible. He cannot get into the lodge without us noticing. His scent is not here." Griffin shakes his head, trying to add logic to whatever the hell has happened.

"Reese, tell me what happened." Ramsey is calm, holding my hand. She is trying to pull me out of the panic spiral that is swirling in my head. I did not even realize that I had fallen to my knees until she sat down next to me and wrapped a blanket around my shoulders.

I take a deep breath, the pain in my head overshadowed by the pain in my chest. "Juni. She sent us a vision. I think. It was like a dream or a memory, but she was looking right at us as she spoke. She was trying to tell us where she was. I don't know how she did it."

"Briggs was there," Bade growls. "He has her underground."

"She said that it was warm, and it smelled weird. Water underground?"

"The springs," Griffin says.

"What? The ones on the way to the lake?" I am trying to focus on what they are saying, but my breaths are still erratic. Bade sweeps me into his arms, the sound of his heartbeats steadying me.

"A little further away, there are underground springs. They are all connected through a tunnel system."

"Would Briggs know about them though?" Griffin asks. "Those springs are in Nightfang and not well known because they are not safe."

I look up and meet Bade's eyes. The worry that I feel is reflected there, swirling with anger.

"We will find her, Wildflower. My brothers and I will deal with Briggs and bring her home."

War and Rowan burst through the door, their babies crying in their arms. We quickly catch them up on what has happened, all of us confused as to how Briggs was able to take Juni but agreeing that the guys would leave right away. The closest entrance to the underground springs system is a two-hour run from here. Once they are inside, they will need to navigate the tunnels to locate her, which could take hours depending on how far into the maze she is being kept.

Feeling helpless, I leave the room, not stopping even when I hear my family calling after me. I walk straight through the lodge, not stopping even when I leave through the front entrance. The cool summer wind blows my hair, strands sticking to the tear tracks running down my cheeks. The sun is just starting to rise. Juni should still be asleep in her bed. I do not stop until I am pounding on the door to the small cabin closest to the lodge. Sylas opens the door, eyes adjusting to the light, confusion pulling his brow as he rubs his chest. My hand is shaking as I grab his wrist, dragging him with me back to the lodge. He is talking. Asking questions. Looking to Ramsey, who followed me outside for answers. When we get back to the front door of the lodge, everyone is standing there looking at me. They approach me as if I am a wounded deer, ready to bolt at the slightest movement.

Bade walks up to stand in front of me, tilting my chin up so that I am looking at his face.

"Sylas can be your map in the tunnels. He just needs to follow the heart string. Juni asked for her Daddy and rubbed her chest. She was telling us that you need him with you. Go get our little girl back." I stretch up onto my toes and kiss my Mate as he wipes the tears from my face.

I turn to my sisters, knowing what I am asking of them. "Briggs will be expecting Bade. He isn't going to hand her back without a fight. We do not know if he is working alone."

"Maybe I should go too," Ramsey says as she turns to Griffin. "If she is hurt…"

He shakes his head. "We will get there faster without riders. Stay with your sisters. We will call Briar and Bree to stay at the lodge while we are gone as well."

"Is that necessary?"

"Heka and Father are helping Arlo and Eden get settled at the outpost. We will all feel better knowing that you have protection while we are gone," War explains.

Bade pulls me into a tight hug, kissing me once more before they leave. My sisters say goodbye to their Mates and before we know it, we are ushered back into the lodge, the door locking us in.

Ramsey leads the way into the living room, carrying Arrow while Ro has Archer and Arden. They mention breakfast and maybe finding some books to read while we wait for an update, but I continue on, walking until I stand before the door leading to Juni's room. Crawling into her bed, neatly made since she has been staying in a different room for the last few days, I curl up and cry.

The air is humid. I am back in the underground springs. I look around, trying to find Juni. Everything around me is tinged in a golden hue and I realize that I am looking through Juni's eyes.

"Stay here and watch her," a gruff voice says from across the room. Briggs is talking to someone else.

"You did not say that there would be a child involved."

"Plans change. We need to draw them out. Once the witches die, their Mates will be weak with grief. Then, we take over. You will be my Beta."

"Where are you going? What if they find us here?"

"They probably do not even know that she is missing yet. She was out sleepwalking when I snatched her."

Sleepwalking? Oh, Juni. She made this happen. A third voice joins the others as they walk further away.

"They left them alone?" Briggs laughs. *"Stay here. I am going to take care of the witches."*

The vision then jumps, showing me different versions, different outcomes. Every possibility flashes quickly through my mind like a movie set on fast forward. My beautiful, brave girl is showing me exactly what we need to do. Exactly what will happen if we stray from the path she has laid out for me.

I jolt awake, my entire body glowing as my moon mark pulses. Rushing into my bedroom, I pull on a bralette and a pair of leather pants, strapping one of Bade's knives around my thigh. Leaving my room, I tie my hair back as I go in search of my sisters.

"Ro, I need you to take the babies up to the Hideaway. We are about to have company, and it is the only way to keep you all safe."

"What do you mean? What is happening?" Ramsey rushes over to me.

"Juni sent me another vision. Briggs is on his way here to try and eliminate us. We are not going to let that happen. Juni showed me how. Ro, hurry. Hide with the babies. I saw many outcomes, and it is the only way to keep them safe. Go, now. We do not have much time."

"I can't just leave you."

"You aren't leaving us. We will be okay. I have seen it. But you need to hide. Protect your babies. Now."

"We can contact the guys, call them back."

I shake my head. "We can't. If they don't stay on their path, Juni will die. I watched it happen." My voice shakes as I recall the vision. "They need to find her now."

"Go, Ro. Take the babies. We will be okay." Ramsey pushes Rowan to the hallway that leads to the hidden room. "Briar! Bree!"

I follow Ramsey as she walks to her room, getting changed into an outfit similar to mine, strapping her knives onto her thighs.

"Is everything okay?" Briar asks as she and her sister enter Ramsey's bedroom.

"Briggs is on his way here." I explain the visions that I saw, stressing the importance of them not contacting our Mates about what is about to happen.

"You should hide, let Briar and I fight Briggs." And I know that they will try. But he will outmaneuver them—overpower them. There is only one option that lets my family walk away from all of this.

"You two need to stay hidden with Ramsey until he arrives. Sneak up on him. Whoever is helping him did not know that you would be here with us. He thinks that we are alone."

"And where will you be?" Ramsey's voice is steady, her training in high stress situations taking over.

"I have my own path that I need to take." Ramsey sees more than I intended in my eyes. "You have to trust me, Rams." After a long pause, she nods her head. "Now, hide. You will know when it is time."

Briar and Bree melt into the shadows. Ramsey gives me a tight hug. "He will underestimate you. Use that." She quickly shows me the best spots to aim for if I need to use the blade on my thigh. "Strike to kill."

I nod, taking deep breaths to steady myself as she disappears deeper into the lodge. I wish that I could tell her what is about to happen. I wish I could prepare her for what we both must do. But she will try to protect me and that cannot happen.

Grabbing a blanket off of the back of the couch, I wrap it around my shoulders and begin pacing. Playing

the part of the distressed, human mother is not difficult.
Based on the light, Briggs should be arriving any minute
now. All I need to do is wait.

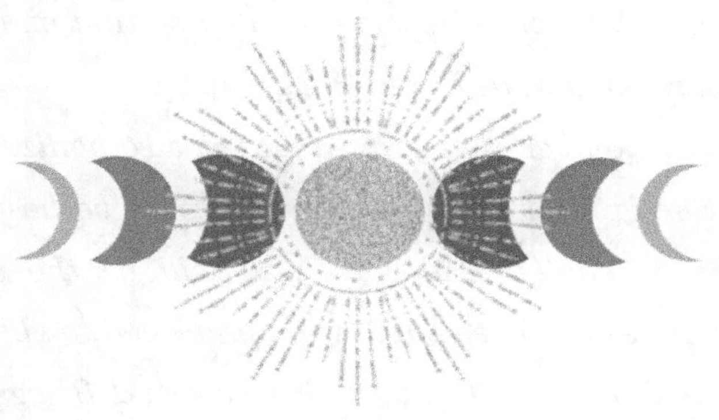

Chapter Twenty-Nine

The trees blur as I tear through the forest. Boone plans to meet us at the entrance to the springs. He asked that we wait to go in until he is there to help, but I made him no promises. Briggs is living on borrowed time, but Juni is my priority.

"We are only a few minutes out from the entrance. Be alert. We do not know if he is working alone. Sylas, you will need to help us find her once we are inside. The tunnels are like a labyrinth, and the walls have been known to cave in. We stick together for as long as we can. Take out any threats and get Juni out safely. Boone does not believe that Briggs would hurt her, but he had no

problems taking her. He is desperate and that makes him even more dangerous," I tell the group.

"*Remember that Juni might not recognize you at first. She is most likely scared and could be hesitant to trust us. Ideally, Bade or Sylas will be the ones to approach her but even then, we might need to shift. She is not as familiar with our wolf forms and Briggs might have used his to intimidate her.*" Griff's reminder has me grinding my teeth. I know that he is right. But the thought of Juni being afraid of us–of me–because of Briggs, it is almost too much for me to bear.

We slow as we approach the entrance, not wanting to barrel in before first knowing how many we will be up against. Using my far sight, I do not see anyone guarding the entrance. I pick up two heat signatures moving around just past the entrance. I do not see Juni. Relaying that information, we decide that War and Griff will go in first, taking out the guards so that Sylas and I can start our search.

Snarls and growls fill the air as War and Griff neutralize the threat.

"*All clear,*" War's words are all I need before I am running. The heat from the springs is making it difficult for me to find Juni through the walls. By the time that we get to our first split in the path, I have to turn to Sylas for help.

"*Which way?*" My words come out with more growl than I intend. Sylas pauses, his wolf trying to find his match.

"*This way…I think.*" Sylas begins jogging down the path that turns to the right.

"*You think?!*"

"*Because she is so young, it is difficult to sense. It is why I did not know that she was taken until Reese woke me up. It is there, though. The pull is there.*"

"*Which means she is still okay,*" Griff adds.

I try to rein in my frustration. My anger is not going to help the situation, and I am grateful for the help that Sylas is able to offer us.

"*The sulfur scent of the springs is getting stronger the further we go,*" Griff tells us. Juni complained about the stinky water in the vision, hopefully we are headed in the right direction.

At every split in the path, we rely on Sylas to lead us. I continue searching for Juni's heat signature but with the heat in these tunnels, it is difficult. Just when I begin to doubt that she is here at all, I detect movement a few chambers ahead.

"Someone is up ahead. It is too large to be Juni, but it might be Briggs. I cannot scent either of them over the smell of the springs."

The tunnels are too narrow in most spots for us to run more than two wide. War and I take up positions in the front while Sylas and Griff stick close behind us. We move as silently as possible, not wanting to alert him of our presence before we are in a position to strike. Creeping forward, we round the bend and enter a large chamber just as rocks fall behind us, sealing us in.

War lunges past me, tackling a wolf to the ground and holding his throat.

"Daddy?" Juni's small voice is one of the best things I have ever heard.

I leap over a pool of steaming water, shifting as I land and fall to my knees in front of Juni. She scrambles into my arms, her skin filthy with sweat and dirt. She has blood on her arm and a wound that is having trouble healing. We are both crying as I pull her tight to my chest.

"You are safe now, honey. We are going to get you out of here." I look around the room, realizing for the first time that the wolf War took out is not Briggs.

"I knew you'd come. I'm sorry I let him take me. It was the only way."

"You had a vision about Briggs? You knew that he would do this?"

"Yes. I'm sorry, Daddy. I had to."

"It's okay, Juni. But now we need to get out of here. Where is Briggs?"

"He left to attack the lodge." Her voice is almost a whisper, but my brothers hear her anyway. Their growls fill the air. "Mommy knows. I showed her as soon as he left."

"Why wouldn't they tell us?" Griff tries to keep his voice calm; despite the panic I know he is feeling while having his Mate in the path of danger.

"It was the only way," she repeats, her body feeling weaker than it should in my arms.

Griff must notice because he comes over and carefully checks the wound on her arm. He brings it close to his nose, trying to smell for infection. His reaction worries me as he pulls himself away and immediately washes his hands off. When he looks over at me, he only says one word. *"Nightshade."*

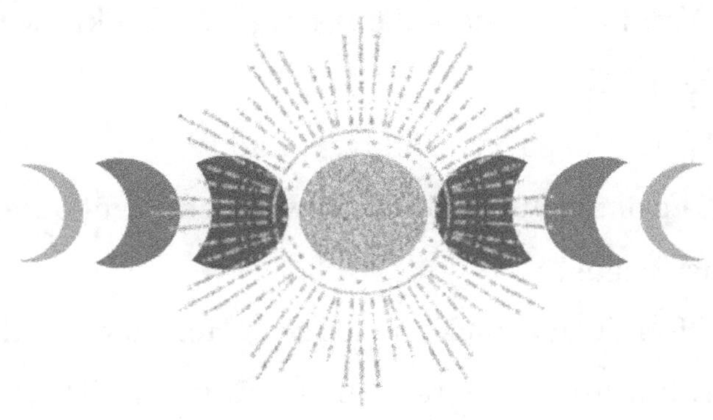

Chapter Thirty

I have never really considered myself a brave person. The craziest thing that I have ever done was allow myself to be captured by Zuri–but even then, I knew that my Viking would save me. I saw it. I guess, in that way, Juni really is like me. But this, well, this could go very badly. This plan is riding on everyone else doing exactly what needs to be done to keep us on this specific path and most of them do not even know what that path is.

If the guys don't find Juni in time, she will die.

If Briggs recruits help on his way to the lodge, we will die.

If Griffin does not scent the poison in Juni's arm, she will die.

If Heka and Lycus return home early, they will die.

If I cannot do what needs to be done, we will die.

Everything must happen exactly as Juni showed me, or my family will not survive this day.

All I can do is wait. Wait for the attack. Wait for the pain.

And hope.

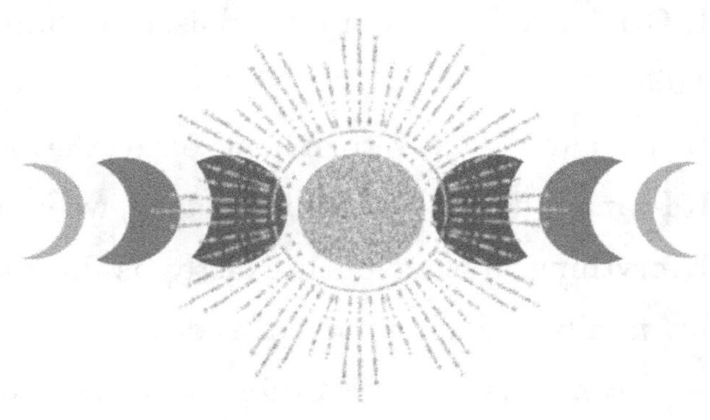

Chapter Thirty-One

Nightshade. Toxic if ingested, it can be fatal to grown wolves–let alone a young child like Juni. Looking closer at the wound, Brigg's intentions are clear. He sliced her arm open and then pressed nightshade into her wound. It will slow her ability to heal. It will weaken her system. If left untreated, she will die.

"When did he do this to you, Princess?" I keep my voice calm and steady. I do not want Juni to know that I am worried.

"Before he left for the lodge, he came back to check on me," she replies weakly. "He saw me glow. He dinnit know I had magic. I clawed at his face, but I wasn't strong enough to fight him. He sliced me with a knife that had somethin' sticky on it and told me that I would see my Mommy and Daddy soon."

She fought back. "I am so proud of you. You have been so brave."

"Can we wash it out? The spring water will be clean even though it smells." Griff will know more about what we can do. We just need to get what we can out of her system.

"It will already be mixing with her blood. We can wash it from her wound, but it will have traveled deeper by now."

"So, what do we do?"

"It needs to be sucked out. But, if any of us swallow it, we will fall victim to the toxins too."

Looking around, I see that War has positioned the body of the guard out of sight. He and Sylas have moved on to try and clear the blocked passage. We do not know how much of the path we took in has been compromised. None of it will matter if I cannot save Juni. War is keeping him busy, but Sylas is struggling to keep his distance, knowing that Juni is in danger.

"Tell me what to do," I tell Griff.

"We need to get out of here. Ro has blocked me. I cannot contact her."

"Ramsey has done the same," Griff groans.

"If we can shift this rock, the rest of the tunnel might be clear," Sylas thought out loud.

"Tell me what to do," I repeat loudly as Juni shivers in my arms.

Turning his attention back to me, Griff curses and then finds a few different vessels, filling one with water from the pool. "You will need to suck the blood out and then spit it out of your mouth without swallowing any down. Rinse your mouth out immediately after. But it is really dangerous. Are you sure..."

"She is my daughter," I growl. "Now, help me hold her while I get this poison out of her system."

Griff runs his hands through his hair before settling himself down beside me and accepting Juni's tiny body into his arms.

"Keep working on the cave in," I tell the others. "As soon as it is clear, we run hard and fast home."

To Griff, I add, *"Promise me you will get her home, even if I am too weak. Get her to Ramsey."*

"You are too stubborn to let a little Nightshade take you out."

"Promise me."

Griff nods. Saying a quick prayer to The Mother, The Moon, and The Sun, I bring Juni's arm to my mouth and suck.

Juni screams.

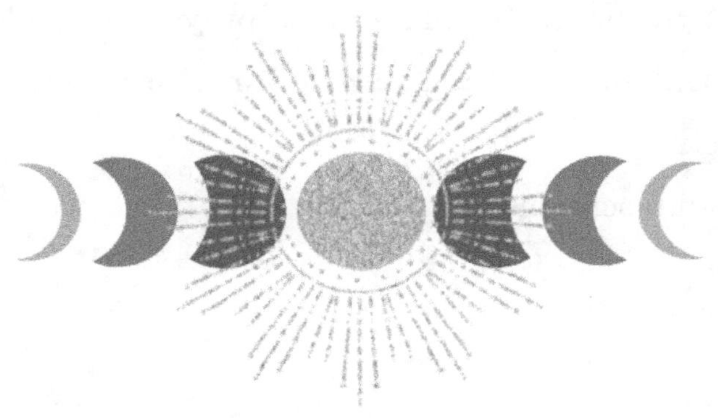

Chapter Thirty-Two

In my peripheral vision, I see him enter the lodge through the garden door. I continue pacing, appearing as if I am lost in my thoughts. I do my best to keep my heartrate steady—my breathing even. He cannot know that I know he is here. Not yet. Once I am sure he has noticed me, I grip my head and crumble to the ground, the blanket hiding the weapon that I hold.

He is in his wolf form, almost identical to Boone but with a painful, festering wound on his face. Claw marks. My brave girl fought back. He snarls and snaps his foaming jaw at me, no longer trying to hide his presence.

He lunges.

Searing, scorching pain burns my back.

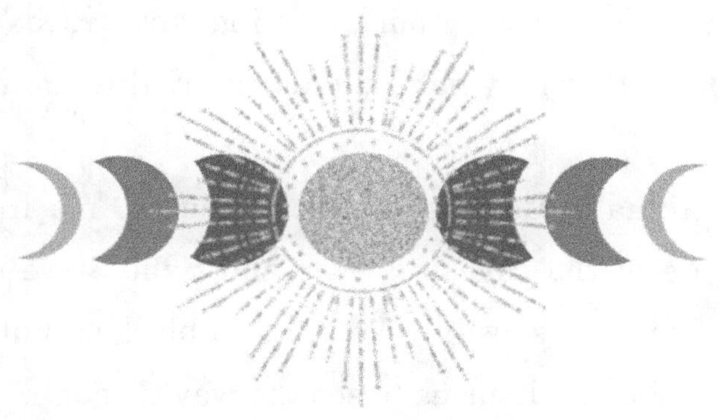

Chapter Thirty-Three

Mouthful after mouthful of tainted blood is sucked out of her body. I spit and rinse my mouth out, refusing to let myself swallow. I am not even sure that I breathe. I can taste the nightshade, a sweet ichor that has mixed with the coppery tang of her blood. Despite Griff's warnings, I do not stop until it is gone. She has lost too much blood—she is weak and cold—but her breathing evens out. Her body's natural healing is able to fight now that the toxins are out of her system.

Turning my head away from her, I see that War has had to restrain Sylas. Hearing Juni's screams was probably too much for his wolf to handle.

I make myself vomit, forcing any traces of the Nightshade that may have slid down my throat out of my system.

"Alpha!" Boone's voice calls out to me from the other side of the cave in. War and Sylas have cleared many of the rocks away. We are still blocked, but a hole has opened enough for us to see the way through.

"In here!" I shout; my voice is raspy from the burn of bile. "Dig the rocks out from your side."

With Boone helping from the other side, the pile of rocks is quickly dealt with.

"Juni." I rub her back, her face—trying to wake her up. "Juniper."

Rubbing her hands on her eyes, she slowly wakes up. "Daddy?"

"You are going to be okay, Princess. But you need to stay awake for me, okay? You need to hold on to my back as we run. Can you do that?"

"I think so."

I smooth my hands over her wild hair, kissing her forehead. "I just need you to be brave for a little while longer." Giving her one more hug, I shift and lower myself down low so that she can climb onto my back.

"Hold his fur as tight as you can," Griff tells her. "We are going to be going really fast, okay?"

War fills Boone in on what has happened while they work together to clear the rest of the rocks. Sylas keeps his distance but looks Juni over to make sure that she is okay now that the toxins are out of her system. I know that his wolf would feel better if she rode with him but can also recognize that she is more comfortable with me.

Once the path is wide enough for us to crawl through, the others shift, and we race home.

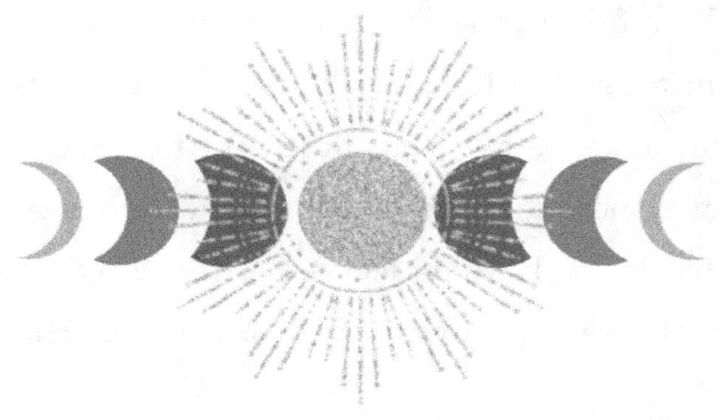

Chapter Thirty-Four

Reese

I am no stranger to pain. But this? This is worse than I have ever felt in my life. I manage to twist my body out of his grip, bringing the dagger up and slicing his side. He is surprised by my attack, but it isn't enough. He snarls and snaps his mouth at my throat. I swipe at him again, making contact before the blade is knocked out of my hand–the crack of my wrist breaking echoes through the air.

Right as he is about to make another attempt at my jugular, he is tackled by Briar and Bree, their wolves biting and clawing at him as Ramsey rushes to my side.

"Let me heal you," she says with tears in her eyes. Her hands are shaking as she places them on my back. My back is in tatters from his claws, and my stomach is bleeding where he bit me. But I will be okay. I saw this happen.

"Not yet," I grit out. "They are going to wound him, but it won't be enough. They will get knocked out. When that happens, you need to use your powers on him."

She looks over to the fighting wolves, dread in her eyes when she realizes that he is overpowering them. "What do you mean? I am not going to heal him."

I shake my head. "You need to make him worse." My words are little more than a whisper as I try to block out the pain. "Make his blood boil. Make his organs deteriorate. Anything that you can picture in that big, beautiful brain."

She shakes her head, "I have never done that before. I don't know if it will work."

"It will. Juni showed me." Tears are freely falling from my eyes, partly from the pain but mostly at the thought of Juni having seen everything that she showed me. My brave little girl who waded through death to find the safest path we could take and then used her power once more to show me what needed to be done.

"We just need to hold out until the guys arrive. They will come back once Juni is safe and they realize that Briggs is here."

"As long as things happen as planned, they are already on their way. But it won't be fast enough. You can do this. I promise."

We look up as we hear a crack—the sound of Bree's body hitting the wall as she is knocked unconscious. Briar's roar pierces the air as she attacks Briggs with renewed strength.

"Bree is okay. But you need to weaken him. Please, Ramsey. You don't need to be the one to kill him, but we cannot win if he remains stronger than us."

Ramsey takes a deep breath and then approaches the fight from Briggs' blind side. Noticing her movement, Briar uses all of her remaining strength to hold Briggs down. He struggles to get out of her control, but it is all the time Ramsey needs to reach her hand out and push her magic into him.

Briggs kicks his legs out, catching Briar's abdomen and slamming her into the wall next to her sister. He snarls and growls, trying to break free from Ramsey's magic but he doesn't have the strength.

Ramsey is sweating and shaking as she wreaks havoc on his body, fighting his natural healing and attacking him from the inside out. The moment I realize that she is going to burn herself out, I crawl to her side and remove her hand from Briggs' body. Touching her hand sends a bolt of pain into my body and she instantly recoils. Taking a dagger from the sheath on her thigh, I use my non-injured hand to press the blade into his throat, slicing deep as a spray of blood splashes against my skin, painting me red as my vision goes black.

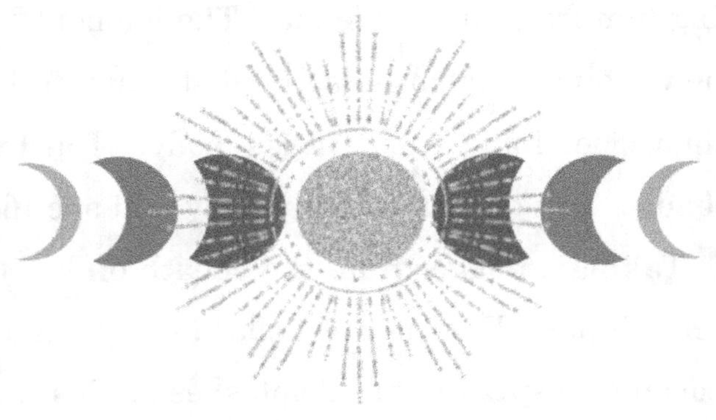

Chapter Thirty-Five

Bade

The scent of blood is thick in the air as we enter the lodge. As soon as I see the scene laid out before me, I shield Juni's eyes, not wanting her to see Reese's lifeless body on the floor.

Ramsey is sitting up, holding her hands to Reese's back as she tries to heal her—but her hands do not glow. She is muttering something over and over. I do not think she has even noticed that we are here.

"Rowan?" War's voice cuts through the ungodly silence as he scans the room looking for his Mate.

"Hideaway," Ramsey rasps, the first sign that she is aware of our presence.

War takes Juni from my arms and leaves the room. The movement jars me from my stagnant state. I rush over to Reese, sliding to my knees on the blood-soaked floor. I sigh a breath of relief when I see that she is still breathing, but her wounds are severe. She is covered in scratches, the deepest being the ones on her back, her wrist appears bent at an unnatural angle, definitely broken, and she has a large wound on her side. I carefully pull her into my arms as tears flood from my eyes. She is breathing. Her heart is beating. She is alive.

"I'm here now," I tell her, tears streaming down my face as I try to stop my fear from taking hold. "Please be okay. Juni and I need you. Please, Wildflower."

Ramsey climbs behind Griff as Boone walks over to Briggs' body, confirming that he is dead and then letting out a quiet sob. His brother was a monster–but he was still his brother. I know that he was hoping it would not have come to this.

I turn my attention back to Reese. "Heal her," I beg Ramsey. "Please heal her."

"I can't," she replies between sobs. "I used it all. I used it to weaken him. Used it to hurt instead of to heal. And now I can't. There isn't enough left."

Griffin soothes her, holding her tight to his chest as she cries.

"Reese saved me. I almost used it all. I almost poured my own life into ending his. She saved me. But I think my magic hurt her. I... I think I hurt her."

"You are going to be okay," Griff tells her. "You will both be okay."

"Reese," I say as I gently tap her cheek with my hand. "Wake up, sweetheart." I lower my mouth to hers, placing a kiss on her lips. "I cannot lose you." My voice breaks as I speak, my mind raging with anger, guilt, relief, pain. My literal heart feels like it is shattering to pieces. I cannot lose her when we just found each other. We are supposed to have forever.

War and Rowan enter the room, carrying bandages and medications. "Sylas is with the kids. Father and Heka are rushing home," War states.

"We need to get Reese clean and bandaged so that she does not develop an infection," Rowan adds. Griff must have updated War. With Ramsey unable to heal her, we need to treat Reese's wounds.

I stand, carrying Reese down the hallway and into our bathroom. A place where, not long ago, we had spent a considerable amount of time cleaning up after our bonding heat. Was that only last night? How is that possible?

Sitting with her on the edge of the tub, Rowan helps me remove Reese's clothes and wets a soft cloth to begin wiping the blood away from her skin.

"She is going to be okay," she tells me. "Reese is stronger than she looks."

"I know she is," I admit. "She knew that this was going to happen. Juni told me that she knew. I am so fucking angry." I am having trouble breathing as sobs wrench themselves from my body.

Reaching over to hold my hand, Ro says, "It is okay to be angry. I am too."

"I almost lost them both today." Both of my girls. My everything.

"But you didn't."

We finish cleaning and wrapping all of her wounds. I set her wrist, and Rowan wraps a splint around it to keep it in place. We pack the deep cuts with the herbs and salves like Heka instructed. The wound on her side is the most dangerous one. Briggs literally bit a chunk out of her. Even with advanced healing, it will be difficult to heal fully. We will not know what damage might have occurred when she interrupted Ramsey's magic until she wakes up and Ramsey's magic returns. Hopefully it will return. It has to return.

"From what Juni told me after you first got back, this was the only way that we all survived. Briggs' initial plan was to attack the lodge during the night, killing me and my babies as we were on one of our nightly walks to rock them back to sleep. When Reese received the second vision, she locked me away with my babies so that we would be saved again. They saved us. Your girls saved us all."

"I just need her to be okay."

"She will be." She squeezes my hand. "But even when her physical wounds heal, she might struggle with what happened. She watched every possible outcome before finding the one that kept us all alive. Juni did too. They both watched us die, over and over. And then, she went up against Briggs—knowing that she would get hurt. Knowing that his death would be on her conscience but being brave enough to do it anyway."

Rowan pulls the blankets back on the bed, helping me arrange Reese so that she is not putting pressure on her wounds.

"I am going to give Juni a bath and make her some food. What would you like me to tell her?"

Juni. Our brave little girl who has had a fucking awful day too. At only 5 years old, she survived a kidnapping, poisoning, and figured out how to save us all.

"Can you bring her here when she is ready? Reese would want her close." She already knows what happened anyway. She saw all of this happen. How can I protect her from any of this when her mind already showed her this nightmare?

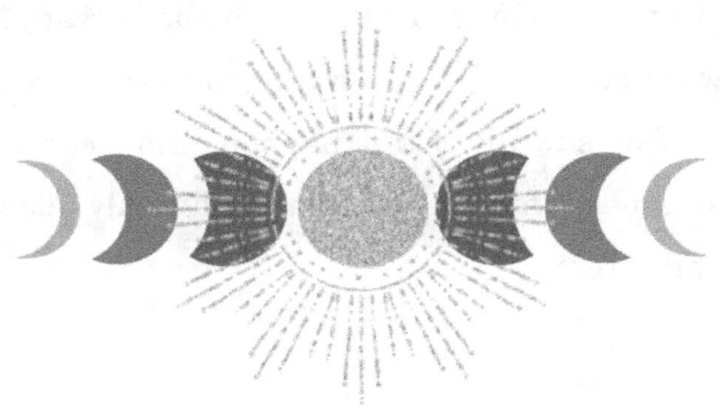

Chapter Thirty-Six

Everything feels heavy. My entire body feels like it was shredded and then stitched back together. Maybe it has. Unable to even open my eyes, I think back on what I last remember.

Panic.

Pain.

Nothing.

Then other memories start floating in.

A deep, calming voice. I clung to his words—allowing them to ground me to this life. My existence is tied to him. My body. My soul.

A woman's voice, filled with love and terror as pulses of warmth filled me, wrapped me up in their light and blasted through the pain.

The warmth of a small body pressed to mine.

I try to sit up. To open my eyes even though they feel like sandpaper.

"Wildflower." That same voice. His voice. "Let me help you." Large hands grip me with so much care, my heart aches to burst from my chest.

His gorgeous face is the first that I see when my eyes finally open. His eyes are heavy, needing sleep that he hasn't been able to find. So blue–like the clearest lake, overflowing with water until it streams like rivers down his face.

"Beast," I whisper.

He gently removes a sleeping bear cub from my side. Our bear cub. Juni.

"I...is she okay?" My voice is little more than a rasp.

Bade places his palm on my cheek. "Yes, she is fine. Our little girl is very brave–just like you."

"What happened?" I ask. My brain is still trying to catch up.

"What do you remember?"

I try to remember what happened before the pain and the nothing. "Briggs." I growl. "He took Juni but then attacked the lodge. She...she showed me how to keep everyone safe. Is he..."

Bade nods. I raise my hands up in front of my face. I did it. I killed him. Fresh tears begin to fall, soaking my face.

"It is okay, sweetheart. You did what you had to. You protected our family."

I let him tug me into his arms. He is careful of my body, making sure not to touch my injuries.

"Ramsey?"

"She is okay too. Her well of magic was emptied— you saved her life by pulling her away from Briggs—and it has been slow to return. Every bit that she gets, she has been using to heal you slowly."

"How long?" I don't need to elaborate. He knows what I am asking.

"Two weeks. You have been asleep for two weeks."

Two weeks? The visions showed me that we would all survive. I knew that I would be injured pretty badly. But two weeks? I thought that I would have healed quicker with my body now able to heal at the rate of a shifter. Everyone must have been so worried.

"When you touched Ramsey's hand, we think that some of what she was doing to Briggs transferred to you. She was able to reverse what was done but it left its mark." He holds my right hand up, bringing it up to his lips before showing me the burn that runs from my palm up to my elbow. Jagged, like a bolt of lightning. "Your other injuries have been healing slowly. The ones on your back have nearly vanished. You will most likely have a scar on your side." Bade gently brushes his fingers over the bandage on my side that I know is covering up a bite wound.

A price had to be paid.

I twine my fingers with his, bringing his hand to rest just below my belly button. "Did... did she check?" I can barely get the words out as Bade's eyes meet mine, surprise flashing in his stare before he shakes his head.

"We haven't." His eyes flash down to my wounded stomach. "Should we?"

I nod my head. "I was shown so many outcomes. So many possibilities. In some, I was able to save all of us. In others—" I shake my head. "A price had to be paid. I tried to shield myself. I tried to make sure that they would be okay."

Bade holds me tight to his chest as a sob barrels out of his chest. "You were so brave, love."

After our tears run dry again, Bade helps me bathe and dress. The wound on my side is now closed, but the edges do look like they will scar. Other than feeling weak, I am thankful that I can move around okay. Juni wakes up and after the longest hug I have ever received, we leave our room in search of food.

We find everyone in the kitchen, bickering over the best bread to toppings ratio for the perfect sandwich.

"I just think that it should have as much meat as we can fit," War says.

"And what if all of that meat that you pulled out can't fit?" Ro asks.

"Then you find a way to make it fit," I reply with a wink. The guys all laugh. Rowan and Ramsey jump up, squealing and pulling me into a hug.

"How are you feeling?" Ramsey asks against my shoulder, tears welling in her eyes.

"Hungry. And exhausted even though I have apparently done nothing but sleep for the last two weeks."

"You did plenty," Ramsey says. "You needed to heal."

Everyone takes their turn in giving me hugs. Heka checks to make sure that my bandage is on correctly and Lycus brings me a slice of cake. When I thanked him and asked what the cake was for, he told me that it isn't a proper celebration without it.

I can't argue with that.

We move into the living room to make ourselves more comfortable and I pause, looking around. Bade slides behind me, wrapping his arms around my middle and resting his head on my shoulder. "Are you okay? We can go somewhere else."

"No. It's...I'm okay. I wasn't sure how I would feel coming back here, but it still feels comfortable. Like home. I don't want one really awful day to take that from me. I still... I don't think that I have fully processed what I did. What I had to do. But I know that I am safe. I know that I am okay." I turn in his arms, bringing his lips to mine and kissing him until we are both out of breath. Pressing his forehead to mine, we stay in that moment for a little longer. "I am scared for this next part, though," I whisper.

"Me too, sweetheart. Together?"

"Together."

He takes my hand in his and we walk over to where Ramsey and Griffin are sitting, eating their own pieces of cake.

"How are *you* doing?" I ask her as I sit down next to her.

She takes a minute to find her words before she answers. "I am okay. The first few days after the attack were awful. I have been having trouble sleeping again. The nightmares..." she shakes her head. "I felt horrible that I hurt you and then did not have the power to heal you right away."

"That wasn't your fault. I am so sorry that I couldn't tell you ahead of time. It was the only way."

"I understand that now. But not being able to heal you. Having you not wake up...it was just a lot to process. Are you sure that you are feeling okay? No weird side effects? Lingering pain?"

I look to Bade for strength. He gives my hand a reassuring squeeze. "Bade told me that your well of magic was empty but it has been filling back up bit by bit. I'm not sure if you have any to spare at the moment but..."

"Is your side bothering you? Or the burn mark? I tried to make both of them go away but I don't think that I can."

I shake my head. "It's not that. I need you to check something...here." I bring Bade's and my clasped hands to my stomach. "I need to know if they survived."

The room around us goes silent. Rowan's sharp intake of breath being the only noise.

After a nudge from Griffin, Ramsey nods, smoothing her hands over her skirt. "Of course."

"I know that you healed her a bit this morning so if we need to wait, that is okay." Bade's words are so tender, I know that she must have struggled during my recovery.

"No. I can check. I'm sorry that I did not think to look before."

"It is so early. I'm not even sure what you would have found before."

Ramsey reaches her hand to press against my bare abdomen. "You shouldn't feel any pain."

I nod my understanding and take a deep breath while I wait for the news. Good or bad, I know that this is just the beginning. I remind myself that Bade and I have each other and Juni. If they are no longer there, we will just try again when we are ready. I repeat those thoughts over and over in my head before I look up to see Ramsey smiling at me.

"They are okay. Healthy. Strong. Their heartbeats are fluttering just as they should be."

A sob bursts from my chest as Bade wraps me in his arms and presses his face to my neck. I can feel his tears wetting my skin as we both shake with the news. A little hand grips onto mine and I turn my head to see Juni looking up at me.

"Happy tears?"

Bade picks her up and pulls her into our hug.

"Happy tears."

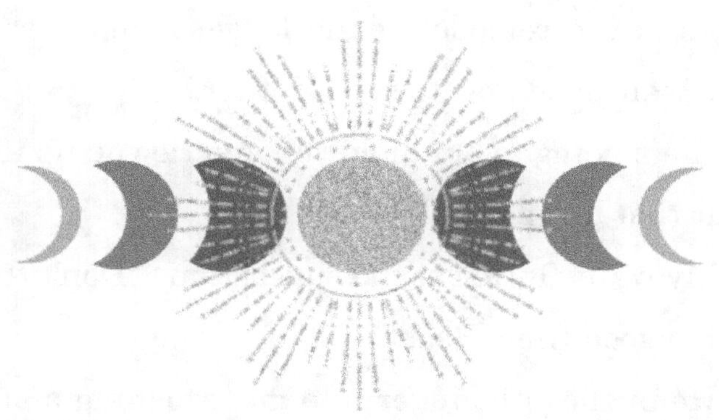

Epilogue

(One Year Later)

Warm lips caress my skin as Bade works his way all over my body. "More," I whisper. He adds teeth, scraping and biting a path to my center, soothing away the sting with his tongue.

We should really be getting ready for the day. Callum, the bear shifter who helped Boone track Briggs, and his clan are arriving at the lodge to celebrate our continued alliance of sorts.

Once the dust settled after the attack, we reached out to Callum wanting to thank him and his clan for their efforts. Due to needing time to heal, the pregnancy, winter, and the remodel of the lodge, it made the most sense to wait until now to get together.

"I am going to blindfold you and tie you up if you do not shut that brain off," Bade warns.

My walls flutter at the suggestion. "Don't threaten me with a good time, Beast."

He pushes his finger into me, groaning as he feels the mess I am already making. "Or maybe I should spank you?" A moan slips out. He chuckles before flipping me across his lap. "Spanking, it is," he growls into my ear as he pulls my ass into the air and firmly smacks, heat spreading across my skin at the pain. Without pause, his hand comes down again. "Suck," he says as he holds a butt plug to my lips. I open my mouth, accepting the toy, as he spanks me another two times.

"You are such a good girl, letting me turn your ass pink." He gathers some of my wetness and brings it to my ass, rimming the ring before working his fingers in, stretching me for the plug. I moan at the intrusion, almost coming from this alone. After one more quick spank, he moves me to my knees at the edge of the bed, taking the plug from my mouth and pushing it into my ass. "So fucking pretty."

"Please, Bade." I whine as I push my ass back into him. "I need you. I need you to fill me."

"I will fill you so full. But first, I need a taste." He drops to his knees behind me, swiping his tongue through my center while playing with the plug. He groans at the taste of me. *"I want to bathe in your sweetness."*

"No complaints here." The words spill from my mouth through my panted breaths.

Bade laughs again, his lips vibrating against my sensitive core.

"I'm so close."

"I know you are, sweetheart. Drench me."

His words send me over the edge. Pleasure courses through my veins as my body writhes under his skillful touch.

Before I recover, Bade pushes into me, filling me completely. I gasp at the feeling, unable to comprehend how it can feel like this every time. The stretch. The heat. The way that he reaches my soul.

"Fuck, Wildflower."

"I know."

Bade pulls me up so that my back is flush with his chest. I reach my hand around, holding onto his neck. He runs his tongue along my shoulder, stopping to bite down on my Mate mark, sending bolts of pleasure throughout my body.

We move together, two bodies moving as one. Two souls aligned.

Feeling his knot press against me, I spin around, wanting to be chest to chest when we lock together. He slides back in, the friction of his knot against my clit pushing me so close to the edge that the edges of my vision go black.

"With me. *Come with me.*" And he does, knotting us together as I clamp down around him. Collapsing on top of me, I let out a tired giggle, squirming under his weight before he tips us to our sides.

"Sorry," he pants.

I laugh again as I bring his mouth to mine in a relaxed, slow kiss.

A loud knock pounds on our door.

"You have about 30 minutes before the bears arrive! You probably do not have time to bathe but for the love of The Mother, please un-attach yourselves before they get here." Griffin's tone is laced with humor.

"Do you think he was just waiting out there for us to finish?" I whisper-yell, knowing that he will be able to hear me if he is still standing by the door.

"Ew. Gross." Griffin replies, causing Bade and I to break out in laughter.

Pulling apart, we quickly clean ourselves up and dress for the day. Leaving our room, we find Rowan and War in the dining room with all of the children—our twins included. Stopping to give Juni a kiss on the head, I take my babies from my sister's arms.

"Thank you for watching them for us. We *very* much appreciate it."

"No problem!" She winks. We have worked out a schedule so that all of us can enjoy 'sleeping in' every now and then.

"Who wants to eat first?" I look down at my little girls. Hazel, our blondie with green eyes, and Ivy, our redhead with blue eyes, each grab at my hair, tangling their little fingers in my curls.

"Briar says they are about 10 minutes out," Bade tells the room. War and Ro encourage the kids to finish their breakfasts, wiping up their faces as they go.

"Eating at the same time, it is!" Sitting down, I hand off Hazel to Bade while I get Ivy settled. Then, I add Hazel back into the mix. This is not our preferred method for breastfeeding, but it works in a pinch.

Ramsey walks in with her hand resting on her slightly rounded belly, Griffin right on her heels.

"Nice of you to join us," he smirks as he fills a plate for my sister.

"Nice of you to eavesdrop." I stick my tongue out at him like the mature adult that I am.

Briar lets us know when they are approaching the lodge. We all file outside, asking Briar to bring them around to the garden where the kids can play while we make introductions.

As far as I am aware, this is the first time that a bear clan has entered the village in over 100 years. Bade does not remember a time when it happened. Curious pack members, in both forms, line the streets welcoming their arrival.

Along with Briar, Boone leads the procession. Everyone is shifted into their human forms, dressed in vibrant fabrics depicting their clan's symbol. Bade steps forward, holding Ivy, as he greets the group.

"Welcome to our home."

The leader, Callum, steps forward to clasp arms with my Mate. "It is nice to finally meet you." Arms still locked together, Callum sniffs the air, gasps, and looks around. Juni comes running towards us, not stopping until she is standing in front of him. "Juniper? But how can this be?"

I step forward, passing Hazel to Bade before picking Juni up into my arms. "Do you know Juni?"

"This is my brother," Juni says quietly. "I have seen him in my dreams, but I didn't know they were *real* dreams."

"I thought you...I came back and everything was burned. Everyone was gone. How did you survive? You were just a baby."

"Your grandmother had a vision and brought Juni to safety during the attack. She raised her alone before she died. And then Juni's heart string brought her to me," I explained.

"These are my Mommy and Daddy now. And my sisters." Juni looks at us with love in her eyes before turning back to her brother.

Callum opens and closes his mouth to speak several times before he settles on what to say. "Can I...can I hug you?" He asks Juni.

"Of course, silly. You are my brother. This is how we were supposed to meet again."

She reaches her arms out, ready to throw herself at him, so I take a step forward to help her into his arms. My arm brushes against his hand and my mark begins to glow. I grasp his hand in mine, not wanting the connection to be broken.

"What's happening?" Callum asks as pictures begin flipping through my brain.

"It's okay, Cal," Juni tells him. "This is the good part."

My powers have developed further in this past year, becoming more detailed than the snippets that I saw before. When the glow spreads to my whole body, I feel Bade step closer, letting out a low growl.

"Stand down," Callum tells his clan. They must have been readying themselves for attack.

The picture becomes clear.

Standing on the banks of a large lake, a young woman with dark hair and pale skin looks out across the water. The light from the full moon reflects off of the snow capped peaks rising out of the ground. A warm breeze tosses her hair around in a wild swirl of midnight.

She has green and gold eyes and wears a Rolling Stones tee with ripped jean shorts. Human.

I repeat the vital details over and over, wanting Callum to have the best chance at finding his Mate. "Bruins Mountains. Large lake. Next full moon. Dark hair. Pale skin."

The vision recedes and I rub my temples.

"What just happened?" Callum asks.

"My Mommy found your Heart Mate," Juni tells him, beaming with pride.

"My Heart Mate? How?"

"My sisters and I are all Moon Touched–just like Juni is Sun Kissed. I have visions, finding True Mates for the wolves in our packs. And, I guess, it can work for bear shifters too. Your Mate is in the Bruin Mountains, near a large lake. She has dark hair and pale skin. She looked scared." I turn to Bade, "When is the next full moon?"

"10 days."

"And how far is that location from here?" I ask Callum.

"About a week, give or take. We could maybe get there sooner but there are warring clans in that area. We may need to fight our way through." He looks back at his clan, all are nodding their agreement.

Rowan walks up next to us, War, Ramsey, and Griffin coming closer as well. "Well, it looks like you guys have just enough time for a good meal and some rest before you have to head back out," she says.

"Is his Mate a shifter?" Ramsey asks quietly. Causing even more confusion to wash over Callum's face.

I shake my head.

"Come inside," War suggests. "We have a wild story to share."

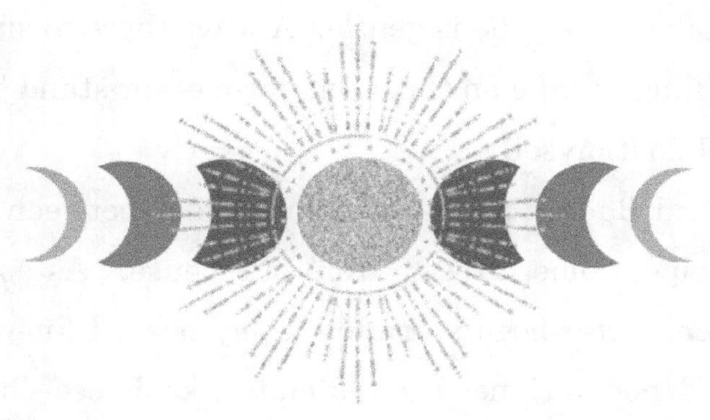

Author's Note

Can you believe that we have already completed The Moon Touched Chronicles trilogy? This entire experience has been surreal for me.

Some of you may know that the Hunt women were characters that I created years ago, but I did not know that they would end up with wolf-shifter, fated mates until after I completed the Nightfang prologue. The bond that the sisters have was inspired by my relationship with my sister.

The Moon Touched men, however, were greatly inspired by my husband.

Like War, he is the provider who loves me exactly as I am—even when I get the crazy idea to become an author.

Like Griffin, he is gentle. Always there to support me. Willing to take on the world for me—or stand by my side as I do it myself.

And Bade? So many of the scenes between Bade and Juniper come directly from our house. As soon as Bade's character began forming in my head, I knew that he would not only need a soulmate like Reese—but he would also need to have a daughter. A little girl who would transform the gruff warrior into a dad who doesn't hesitate to put on a tutu and tiara for a tea party.

Thank you so much for going on this journey with me. It means more to me than I will ever be able to properly convey with words.

The Nights may have found their happily ever after—but there are more stories to be told from the shifter world. Keep reading for an excerpt from The Sun Kissed Scrolls: Lightclaw.

Prologue

(25 Years Ago)

"Sleep well, little one. Tomorrow when you wake, you will be another year older." My Nana's voice soothes me while I snuggle into my warm bed.

"Will I get a special mark like you?" I reach my hand out to trace the Sun Kissed marking that decorates my Nana's face.

"No, love. You will not receive a Sun Kissed mark. But you are just as important to our family line. One day, when you are older, you will protect our family line and ensure that the Sun Kissed blessings remain in the next generation of Claw bears."

"I will?"

"Yes. I have seen it." She places a kiss on my forehead before turning to leave my room at our keep.

"Are you sure I won't get a mark?" I try to keep the disappointment out of my voice, but she hears it anyway.

Nana walks back over and kneels beside my bed. "The females in our family wear a golden mark as proof of their power. But you, my dear grandson, have power in here." She places her hand over my heart. "Your heart holds the greatest power of all. Stronger than any other magic."

"Will my heart sing like father's?"

"Yes. And when it does, you must listen to it."

Nana's voice begins to sing a haunting lullaby, spinning a tale of pain, bravery, and love. I let the words sink into my soul as I drift off to sleep.